Warning

GAY DRAMA WITH HEA

Gay Fiction / Mature-Bear Romance / Paranormal Ghost Mystery / Family Drama / Long Time Lovers / Lumber Jacks / Adult Content / Heat Level 4

This book contains varying degrees of explicit homosexual scenes and adult language. It is intended for sale to adults ONLY, as defined by the laws of the country in which you made your purchase. Please store your files wisely, where they cannot be accessed by under-aged readers.

POSSIBLE TRIGGERS

Language / Drama / Explicit Sexual Content

DEDICATION

To my other half, Talon ps:

Every day is a struggle to go on without you, my twin.

Every word I write is because I promised you I would keep going, and I

would finish all the books we started together.

But you cheated with this one. It wasn't on the list.

TRADEMARK ACKNOWLEDGEMENT

Following Trademark &/or copyrighted name brand products have been either mentioned or used fictitiously in this story.

Movies:

UP! – Walt Disney Pictures & Pixar Animation Studios

Brokeback Mountain – River Road Entertainment and Focus Features

Finding Nemo – Walt Disney Pictures & Pixar Animation Studios

Misc:

CF-AYO La Premier Norseman

Castle

Sons of Anarchy

Nathan Fillion

Lumberjack World Championship

ESPN

THEIR PLANE FROM NOWHERE

TARIAN P.S.

THEIR PLANE FROM NOWHERE

THE TEDDY BEAR COLLECTION
TARIAN P.S.

Gay Fiction / Mature-Bear Romance / Paranormal Ghost Mystery / Family Drama / Long Time Lovers / Lumber Jacks / Burn Level: Cruising / Heat Level 4 / Always Been Always Will HEA

In their small town in the Pocono Mountains, Earl Knox and Hank Grisset have never been considered among the pretty ones to anyone but each other. As lucky as Hank and Earl consider themselves to have found each other, that's about as far as luck has gone. All those Could'ah— Should'ah— Would'ah— moments a man never sees comin', but that don't stop him from regrettin' them later in life.

When Earl makes a critical decision that ultimately outs him and Hank, a mysterious plane shows up at their lake house.

Coming out in a small town can erase friendships in a heartbeat. But when a rift in the family leads to a life-threatening accident, only their devotion and love for each other is gonna get them through this— that, and their plane from nowhere.

TABLE OF CONTENT

1

Earl Knox pulled his truck down along the graveled driveway and parked alongside the mountain lake home. A quick glance not seeing Hank's truck told him he weren't round yet— most likely gone into town to pick up a few odds and ends for the weekend. Course, Hank could'ah called and Earl would'ah stopped— and such was the phrase of most of their life, it seemed. *Could'ah— Should'ah— Would'ah—*

Could'ah come out of the closet long ago—

Should'ah not gone out on that date his folks forced him on—

Would'ah been happy with it being just him and Hank.

But that's not how their story goes. Instead, they were living their own version of *Brokeback Mountain.*

Earl hopped out of the truck, dragging his overnight bag along with him. *Hop* being the nonoperative word. At his age, *hop to it* was something that his body just didn't do. Though he'd been a foreman of the Pocono Mountain Mill and Tree Works for some time now, he was also a born –n- bred lumberjack, and you both *hopped to it* and *got the fuck out of the way*, pronto. 'Bout the only two phrases he or any of the boys who worked for him knew. That and a large array of colorful curse words, including a few custom-made ones.

Earl took his things and followed along the well-worn footpath, down the side of the house heading for the porch when he came to a dead stop—

"Huh." He scratched at his head a moment at the sight. "And where the hell did you come from?" Earl glanced around, seeing nothin' else particularly out of place. He spotted the lawnmower— still the same old, rusty thing as it was. The broken-down wheelbarrow— even the footpath he was standing on still had no stonework. *Okay, so, no surprise lottery win here,* but then Hank was gonna have some heavy explainin' to do about the airplane that was sittin' in the water at the dock.

He tossed his bag up on the step and then wandered down the hill to the dock to have a closer look. He really didn't know much about planes in general let alone water-skipping ones. But he could still size her up a bit just from looking at her: a single prop engine sittin' on oversized pontoons. Nothin' fancy, she was still just her naked aluminum body save for a bright red stripe down her side— and she was beat all to Hades and back. The last couple of numbers on her tail section were worn off, and her windows were coated with a heavy grime, making it impossible to see inside the cab. *Old* was an understatement. *He* was pushing old; this thing was old *and* rundown. So, what the hell was it doing here? And at *their* dock?

Earl reached out to touch the wingtip and got a shock that had him snapping his hand back fast. "Seems you got some serious electrolysis goin' on there. You sure won't be lastin' long if we don't getcha fixed up quick." He stepped back, just looking her over and scratched over the small bit of salt 'n' pepper chest hairs that peeked out from the top of his shirt. He then ran his fingers through a thick mop of matching hair on his head as he stood there still looking her over. His head filled with nothing but more questions and not one conclusion.

While he still expected Hank to explain this, he could see them both havin' some fun with it, too.

"Sure hope Hank knows how to fly one of these." He chuckled and headed back for the house to fetch a toolbox.

Earl liked workin' on things, and he often spent his weekend escapes up here fixin' this or that, includin' Hank's personal plumbin'. He liked doing that, too. And *just on weekends* wasn't near enough to satisfy his *Hankerings*—

He went back up the path around back to the garage and pulled the door open. Right away, he noticed a few things had been moved about and the toolbox he was wantin' wasn't in its normal spot. "Must'ah got put in the barn shed." Earl rolled the garage door closed and headed down the long trail that crossed over ways to the far end of the four-acre lot.

The lake house was theirs. Their home away from everything that tried to keep them apart. Hank had gotten it from his Uncle William, the only man in Hank's life who knew about them and didn't have a problem with it. When Will passed away, he'd left the mountain lake home to Hank to get away from it all. 'Cept Hank struggled to keep hold of it. It weren't no cheap thing to live up in these parts.

Earl had tried to help, but he was screwed up tight with a wife he never wanted. All because of that girly-date he *should'ah not done* a lifetime ago which had landed him gettin' blamed for knockin' her up. And no amount of *"I never touched her"* counted for anythin'. The parent war on both sides of the fence had them both gettin' shoved down the *I do* aisle just as the baby bump started to show. At least the next three bumps were actually his. He'd had them tested to be certain, and they were great kids. He loved every one of them, including the first, who turned out to be the product of Nelson Bronson, the rich kid who just wanted a taste of the Pocono locals while he and some of his college buds were up for some ski runs and then some. Nevertheless, as far as Earl was concerned, that child was his own; loved him just as much as the others, and only he knew the truth. However, throughout the years of raising his kids and watching them grow up, he and Gracie remained strangers, and still the damn woman refused to let him go. When she'd had her tubes tied after their daughter was born, his baby-makin' days were over. So was the act that made them. She' never much liked him no ways. He'd been her emergency *get-out-of-trouble plan* that backfired on her terribly. But that first time he rejected her, she hated him, and has never let him forget it ever since.

He let Gracie run the house, but when his folks died, he took every penny of his inheritance and gifted it to Hank. Gracie couldn't say one word about it: served her right for not givin' him the divorce when he'd asked for it. The night he'd happened upon makin' that request, she'd threatened to take his pension and everythin' they had. What was worse was she swore she'd see to it the kids would hate him. It was then he decided while he may be stuck with her, he wasn't going to skimp on his trips to be with Hank either, anymore. So instead of a one- or two-week getaway every other month, it became every weekend. Been that way ever since. She wouldn't dare out him, and he made damn sure to remind her that if the lumber mill were made aware he was gay, they'd fire his ass on the spot, and then she'd have nothin'. Not even his pension.

Earl'd hated for a long time. Never in his life had he wanted to wrap his fingers 'round another's neck and shake it so hard as he did then. She had him by his nuts, but at least he had her by her tits in return. Still, it pissed him off to no end that they should have to stay this way on account of money or the loss of his kids' love. She didn't like him any more than he did her, so why bother to stay miserable? He'd left that night after their feud and come to stay up here with Hank for three weeks, until Hank made him go back. They both agreed they didn't have enough tucked away to cover them both. And of course, Hank went back home to Emma.

At least there, Hank's trapped life wasn't entirely about hate. Hank was the run-of-the-mill Southern Baptist good ol' boy who hid his gay side 'cause the church folk and his good-hearted, lovin' parents expected him to. Emma was the cute button-nose girl down the street with scratched-up shins and dirty knees on account she was as much a tomboy as she was a southern girl with blonde pigtails. She'd always had a crush on Hank, and he used hers to hide the fact *he* was crushin' on Johnny Davenport, the town's bad boy with a souped-up Vitamin-C Orange Plymouth Superbird. 'Cept Johnny turned out to be a *real* bad boy.

Hank happened to come across Johnny down at the creek one day with none other than Emma pinned under him. Hank beat the living tar out of Johnny and became forever Emma's hero. A few years later, Hank married her.

How, years after, Hank and Emma wound up here in Scranton, Pennsylvania, in the Pocono Mountains, Earl still couldn't imagine, but he was glad of it. Ever since their first encounter at the country fair when he laid eyes on Hank, he was most certainly glad of it.

Hank got himself a job in the millworks, and Emma worked as a housekeeper at the nearby resort during ski season. Thursday nights was family night for most Scranton folks, but Friday and Saturday soon became Hank and Earl's. No one even noticed; the local whiskey hole was full up of guys wantin' to drink and get away from the family— *namely the wife.* And to just hang out with like kind. Just wasn't likely for the same reason as he and Hank did. But that's how their story began.

Earl made it to the barn shed and swung both doors open wide to let in the light. A Barn owl, who'd been livin' up in the rafters for goin' on three years now, chirped his disapproval with the intrusion of sunlight.

"How's it goin', Hoot?" Earl called up to the owl as he walked in. That's what he named it, on account of he and Hank not bein' all that creative when it came to pet names. They'd had a Labrador once, and after a week of not comin' up with anythin' they could agree on, they just called him *Dog.* Dog wagged his tail and that was that.

Earl spotted his toolbox amidst a few of Hank's things scattered on the old wooden workbench. Hank had obviously been up to somethin', but so far, the resulting productive evidence eluded Earl. He spotted the meter gauge hangin' on the pinboard, grabbed it, and headed on back down to the dock and the new arrival.

Hank lived here full time now. Emma had passed away a few years back, and since then he'd been tryin' his hand at bein' a writer. Earl figured it was his way to gain some closure for all the shit they'd been through, still managing to hang on to each other. Life for them had changed so drastically shortly after they'd gotten the lake house. Hank had finally come out to Emma about them, and she'd taken it surprisingly well. Only, her little-girl crush which she still had, was hurtin' from it. She'd even told him she would give him a divorce if he asked for it, and he'd spent the better half of a year thinkin' it over. He'd finally decided to set them both free— their two boys were nearly grown-up, so no sense in draggin' it out. Then one night while Hank and he were up here, they got a call from the local sheriff's department. Emma and the boys had been in a car wreck. They'd lost control in the rain and their van went down the side of the ravine. The boys didn't make it, and Emma was barely hangin' on.

After that, asking for a divorce just wasn't in the books. Earl had even suggested Hank move them both up to the lake house. And for a while there, it was the three of them: Emma and her two men. They'd both been at her side holdin' her hand when she'd died shortly after having a stroke. She'd thanked Hank for stayin' just to keep her company. Hank cried 'cause he did actually love that little tomboy southern girl.

Now, it was just Hank and him, and Earl's thorn back at the house. Gracie was havin' an affair with someone he cared not knowin' too much about. The four kids were all grown up now and off on their own.

This was their story. No romance novel here and certainly neither one of 'em was no pretty boy. Well, maybe Hank's boyish southern face, even at his age, he had that Sundance kid Robert Redford look about 'em. But Earl's face at 54 wasn't likely to make it on any one of those gay websites they found themselves lookin' at from time to time, while Hank made friends with other up-and-comin' authors. 'Course, Hank kept tryin' to tell him he was going to use their pictures for his book cover, and Earl 'course told him, *"Don't no one want to look at an old bear like me"*. Hank's response every time was, *"I do*". And that, of course, was enough to melt Earl's ol' lumberjack heart.

The path opened up to the lake yard. There she was, sitting down at the dock looking as ugly as can be, and yet Earl was falling hard for her already. He decided to grab a towel from his truck right quick before going down.

He returned, coming down the side of the house, glancing up as he came around the corner, just like earlier when he'd arrived, and once more coming to a screeching halt. The toolbox in his hand dropped, crashing and spilling its contents around his feet.

He just stood there stock straight, wide-eyed he was sure of— 'cause there was no way in all hell a plane could just get up and walk away— but sure as shit—

It was gone.

2

Hank Grissett pulled in right behind Earl's truck, his fingers on the wheel went from tapping to the country music to tapping nervously.

Shit.

"Well, you knew you were gonna have to tell him somethin'—" he scratched at his upper lip a moment, "but what?" *Well, he didn't have any screwy idea what,* but there was no puttin' it off. He'd known the moment he discovered it at the dock, he was gonna have some 'splainin' to do. Made it worse when he called the sheriff to come take a look and the damn thing'd disappeared on him just before they arrived.

Jerrod was probably the youngest on the sheriff's force, and he just gave Hank that look like he were on drugs or somethin'. "Did Thomas put you up to this?" Jerod had asked.

"Huh? Thomas? No, I uh—" Hank glanced back to the vacant spot of water next to the dock, then back at Jerrod, blinkin' several times as he was unsure of just what to say.

Jerrod rolled his eyes. "Okay, Hank. Joke's on me. Next time, wait 'til I'm off duty and find somethin' that's actually funny to pull a prank with."

Hank pursed his lips in, decidin' it was his only way out. "Yeah, well it sure did sound funny in my head when I thought of it."

"Uh-huh." Jerrod obviously wasn't amused.

Hank scratched his head and shrugged at him, giving the sheriff that dumb boyish look Earl said he was good at, and scratched his head for a good five minutes. Then just stared down at the empty dock while the sheriff cruiser pulled out.

The next mornin' she was back.

Hank didn't bother callin' the sheriff back over that time. Weren't no way he was gonna puttin' himself through that again. That was Tuesday, last week.

Earl's usual Friday return home was interrupted when his baby-girl became a momma after tryin' for four years and went into labor that Friday mornin'. Earl had kept Hank up-to-date, includin' the news she had delivered a healthy preemie grandbaby Saturday mornin'. So, no beans about it, Earl had to stay behind.

Hank sure did miss him. Earl wanted him to come down, but that Gracie had been in one right sour mood, all 'cuz Leanne had called her daddy first, and it'd miraculously slipped her mind all together to call her momma. Hank had decided to keep his distance. But Earl fed him pictures on the cell phone all afternoon to make him feel like he was there anyhow. He'd nearly cried when he laid eyes on their Leanne's first baby. Okay, so maybe he *actually* cried a tad.

Earl had never told the kids he and *Uncle* Hank were actually a gay couple, though they figured the kids would'ah done figured it out by now. It hurt not bein' able to be open about it to them; then again, not confessin' openly spared the kids havin' to listen to Gracie rage about *her* opinions as well. So far, she had no one to gripe about it to, so it had some payoff. Sometimes it was best not to let the cat out of the bag after all.

Well, Hell's fire, he couldn't sit here in his truck all day.

He got out, grabbing the box of tools and groceries from the back, and headed down the path. He peeked through the trees down the yard, unable to make out the wingtip for the plane, and he felt a weight drop from his nervous gut— *maybe she wouldn't come back until after Earl went back home—* then maybe he'd have a little more time to figure—

He came to a stop when he found Earl's toolbox and contents scattered on the ground. "Shit." He glanced down at the dock at what *wasn't* there and shook his head. Guess Earl must'ah saw it and then didn't. Only thing Hank could do now was just go in and play it like nuttin' weird was goin' on. *Hell's fire.*

Hank never even made it inside, finding Earl sitting on the porch swing, just staring like he'd seen a ghost. Which he kinda had if'n he saw the plane before it vanished. Yet, Hank couldn't help but find him sexy lookin' right then and there too, even if'n he was all stupefied in his expression. Just somethin' about Earl's salt-n-pepper hair and matchin' scruff. Earl was a big feller, too. Big hammer-size bones and lots of meat on them. *Grrrrrr—* his very own *Paul Bunyan* bear.

Hank set the box down next to Earl's overnight bag, still sittin' on the stoop, and went over to join him, forcing on his all-casual-nonsense grin as best he could.

"Hey, babe." Hank leaned in, kissing him, and then purposely sat with his back to Earl so he could lay back over Earl's lap, wiggling his brow. "Feel like some make-up sex, babes?"

Earl didn't respond and, *well,* that just weren't gonna do. Hank reached up and slowly undid the buttons of Earl's plaid shirt. Pretty much all he ever wore— flannel in the winter and lightweight cotton somethin-or-other in the summer, like now. Today's colors were light blue broad lines with gray pinstripes. *Mmmm, gray,* he thought as he swept Earl's shirt aside with his fingers to expose all the dusky-gray and black chest hair. Then without a moment's hesitation, he snatched that pink man-nipple peekin' out from that curly goodness and gave his bear a solid pinch.

"OUCH! Hey, now!" Earl woke from his daze, his hand sprang up to guard his nip from his attacker, "Ow, watch it." He dropped his gaze, seeing Hank for the first time like he'd magically appeared just like something else had disappeared. Hank had that boyish gonna-get-in-trouble look about him, which meant he was up to something. It was that very look he wore the day they met. Earl'd fallin' for it instantly, and he was lovin' every bit of bein' in a heap-o'-mess with Hank ever since.

"So— uh— what's new?" Earl tried hard not to do a look down toward what weren't there, but he wasn't so sure he succeeded. He did, after all, see a plane sitting at the dock there earlier. He'd even touched it.

Hank shrugged with a wiggle that made a quiver across his lips. Earl growled— weren't no sense puttin' up a fuss 'bout what they couldn't see, but he wasn't gonna let it go forever either. Hank knew darn well what he was askin'— just playin' dumb for whatever reasons— and he wanted to know about it. But first, he wanted some of those lips. He scooped his southern strawberry blond up in his arms and hefted him up for some good ol' make-up kissin'.

"Mmm, missed you somethin' awful," Earl mumbled against Hank's lips. "Dja'eet yet?"

"Nah, just waitin' on you." Hank went back to playing with Earl's wounded nipple, thumping it several times with the pad of his finger 'til Earl got the tickles and squirreled away from him.

"Why didn't'cha call me? I could'ah swung by the store and got whatever you needed."

"I had to go pick up a special order for our grandbaby, so since I was in town I went ahead and hit the grocers, and then the hardware store while in town."

"Uh-huh and what'cha get at the hardware store?" Earl's eyebrows went to the top of his head on that one.

"Nuttin' really."

"Uh-hmmmm," Earl mumbled. "So how much you spend on little baby Crystal?"

"Twice more'n what we agreed on." Hank grinned like a naughty man.

"Hank, why do we talk about these things if you're just gonna do somethin' else?"

"Hey, it's Leanne's first. She deserves it. Besides, that little girl is cute as can be. Looks like you. How could I resist?"

"She does look like her ol' grandpop, don't she?" Earl beamed proudly.

Hank put on the biggest grin for his man and nodded just as proud as Earl himself. "So, you feel like a swim before we eat?" Hank was bolting up and ready.

"Are you serious?" Earl pointed down to where—

He caught himself, thinkin' better of it before saying somethin' that would make him sound like a lunatic and made a disgruntled face— his finger still frozen, pointing to where there weren't nothing' to be fussin' over. "Not particularly." Earl gruffed out his response, dropping his hand.

"Sure?" Hank asked, pretendin' he didn't know what had Earl all buggered-over as he pulled his shirt over his head, dropped it to the porch deck, and then toed his sneakers off. He put on the boyish grin again, realizin' he had Earl's attention now. Even if'n his bear were still reluctant to go down to the water. *Hell's fire.* Hank unbuttoned his fly and dropped his drawers right there, and then shoved his boxers down with 'em and clumsily stepped out. He liked how Earl was makin' some adjustments, but what Hank really wanted was Earl nekkid right alongside him— *or on top of him*— *or behind him.* Hell, about any ol' way, so long as Earl was butt nekkid and in that water here soon. Hank shrugged and padded on down the steps and headed for the lake below.

"Ya know, your ugly pecker ain't that temptin'!" Earl hollered out to him.

Hank didn't even look, just reached behind, grabbed both his ass cheeks, and pulled them apart a couple of times, giving his man a cheeky show. "Wanna bet?!" Hank dared him, and when he made it down to the dock, he took a running jump, and dove into the lake.

He swam out a ways, rolled to his back, and looked up toward the house, watching as Earl came trundling down the sloping yard striped down nekkid just like Hank wanted him to be. He quickly kicked around to head back to the shallows to make himself available as a reward.

He swam in just as Earl was arriving hip deep in the water, scooping up water by the handful and splashing it over his chest and shoulders, washing away the day's heat. Except Hank was gettin' some gears goin' about establishin' some fresh new heat between them. He swam in close, keeping low in the water, and slid his hands up Earl's legs. He glanced up with what he hoped was his best wicked look, "I'm thinkin' I am in the mood for some nibblin' on your da-donk-a-dunk." Hank wriggled his brows up at Earl.

"Don't be chewin' on my noggin. My bits are tender."

"Oh yeah? How tender?"

"As in, *my one-eyed, purple-helmet, yogurt-soldier is in dires for some fireworks*, tender."

Hank got the hint right away. He took a deep breath and submerged his head down under the surface. He fumbled a moment finding Earl's half-hard cock, and like magic, he got it in his mouth without losing but a few precious bubbles of air. Hank liked those first couple of seconds before Earl's length was fully erect. He enjoyed rollin' the tender flesh around on his tongue with a *nom-nomming* suction. Except it never lasted long. Within a minute, Earl's cock was a throbbing stiffy in his mouth and the vocalized approval being announced over his head was anything but shy. Of course, Hank wasn't Aquaman, so a few minutes was about all he could do before he had to finally let Earl go and come up for air.

Hank came up with a loud gasp, sucking in a deep breath to refill his lungs and went to work plastering the fuzzy chest with some attention.

"Ya know, you can't be messin' with my pecker like that and then just leave me hangin'," Earl complained.

Hank stood up then, reaching out to fondle Earl's *said* pecker just under the water's surface. "Hmmm, doesn't seem to be doin' much hangin' right now."

"It still needs more attention." Earl's hands dropped around him, pulling Hank's body against him. Eager cocks crashed together as Earl's hands reached around Hank's body, teasing his backside some before taking both their dicks in hand and stroking them together.

"Ahh, yeah, that's how I like my big bear," Hank growled out, coiling an arm around Earl's neck and pulling him down for some long-awaited kissing.

Earl steadily pulled at both their dicks with one hand while his other hand shifted Hank around to a slight angle where he could reach for some extra fun.

Hank felt the thick finger sliding over his tight pucker— teasing him. "Mmm, damn. Don't suppose you brought a bottle of lube down with you?" Hank asked, against Earl's neck, findin' he was havin' to work to catch his breath again as that fat digit circled his hole. He pushed back, eager to move past the toyin' and get on with the doin'.

"I was rather occupied watchin' your ass struttin' down here for a swim, and all the blood left my brain to go to my pecker, so— no, I wasn't thinkin' after that." And then Earl pushed a finger in.

"Mmmm," Hank groaned, his hips swaying forward and back between Earl's hands, one pumping his cock, the other pushing a finger slowly into his hole, crooking it, and catching him just right. A few more pumps and he was ready to spill that fast. His forehead crashed against his lover, huskin' out his enjoyment with each breath, and then it came— *or he did, rather.* He let out a pained growl and then a shiver trailed down and right back up his spine, makin' his knees bob underneath him as he felt his cum fire off from his cock. Earl's release was right behind him— the distinctive groans alerted Hank. He quickly dropped back down below the water's surface and sucked Earl's cock into his mouth, adding a swirling caress of his tongue to Earl's handiwork, until Earl unloaded on his tongue.

When Hank's body started rebelling for lack of oxygen, he bobbed up through the water to stand in front of Earl. However, the expression on Earl's face wasn't the one he should'ah been wearin' after the power suck job he just got. Instead, it was one that had *ghost story* written all over it. Obviously, Earl was seein' their ghost plane again as he was standin' rigid as a formaldehyde corpse gawpin' at somethin' just over Hank's shoulder.

Hank stilled, pursing his lips a moment, then scratching at his upper lip wishin' there was some way he could stall this. "It's back, isn't it?" He asked reluctantly.

Earl's head just barely rocked up and down.

"You seein' an airplane just behind me?" Hank quizzed.

Again, Earl nodded. Hank didn't look. He wasn't so sure he wanted to look, not this close anyways, or while bein' in the water with it at the same time. So, he just waited. He knew the questions would be comin'. Wouldn't do no good to ask though, he still didn't have an answer for not one of 'em.

"You got some explainin' to do."

"Yeah, so uh— you gonna tell me how I'm supposed to 'splain an airplane that comes and goes, but not by any normal plane-flyin' kinda way?"

"Where'd it come from?"

Hank shrugged. "How'm I supposed to know that?"

"When was the first time you saw it?"

"Tuesday, last week?"

"Why didn't you call the sheriffs? What if it's one of them drug planes or somethin'?"

"I did call. I thought the same thing."

"And?"

"And they thought I was the one on drugs or pullin' a prank."

"You mean it weren't here when they did come out?"

Hank nodded. Earl's eyes never left the hulkin' crumble of steel floatin' just behind him. Question after question, the same questions Hank already anticipated, seein' he'd asked himself the very same ones himself. *Several times over.* Yet as simple as the questions seemed, the answers weren't.

"So, when'd it come back?"

"Next mornin'. She was sittin' right back where she is, same thing as now."

"So why didn't you call them back?"

"And say what, Earl?" Hank raised his hands up, locking his fingers and landing them down on his head. "Hey Jerrod, you know that plane I said was here, but weren't when you arrived? Yeah, well, it's back."

Earl scratched over his chest a moment, pushing his lips out like a duck while he thought it over. "Yeah, alright you got me on that one." Not taking his eyes off the plane, he reached out, taking Hank by the shoulder and corralled him out of the water— just in case— 'cause— *well 'cause this was just too freakin' weird.*

Even as they showered and got their evening meal prepared, no amount of trying to keep preoccupied prevented either of the two men from occasionally glancing out the window to see if the plane was, in fact, still there.

Earl shoveled into his mix of potatoes and corn and followed it with a large chunk of meat ripped from the country ribs. He'd purposely sat opposite his normal spot on the table with his back to the dinin' room window so he wouldn't be lookin' at it. But it was there— that and a whole heap of crazy nonsense questions. He was beginnin' to lose his appetite over it. He finally gave up and dropped the fork to the plate. Not even the spicy vinegar aroma of the Canadian family-recipe barbeque sauce could convince him to pick it back up. He parked his heavy arms on the table just starin' down at his plate without actually seein' it. Askin' all those damned questions in his head— *where'd it come from— who'd it belong to— how'd it just vanish and come back like that— was he goin' senile—*

He finally glanced up with one of them questions steepin' on the tip of his tongue, but he refrained, seein' the way Hank was lookin' at him. Earl was worryin' the hell out of him already. Earl was a simple man, grew up around these small mountains; his world was made up of simple townsfolk and loggin'. He watched just enough sports and news to share friendly conversation with the boys at work, reckonin' not one of them would be all too interested in gay pride and all that. *Dammit.* He sucked in a deep breath and let it out in a heavy huff that flared out his nose. His mind was in such a rut. Just that one stupid thought beat him down that he didn't even have the balls to stand up for his own rights for equality seemed to stamp some kinda dogma on his life. Like he needed one more thing to make him feel miserable about all the poorly *should'ah-could'ah-would'ah* choices he'd made.

At least this past week he finally made a good one for him. And for Hank.

"I seem to have lost my appetite, Hank. Whad'dah say we just toss the table scraps out for the critters and curl up for some TV?"

Hank didn't lose his wrinkled face for a second, but he forced on his boyish smile for him, grabbed up the plates, and toted them into the kitchen. *Gawd, he did love that man.* Earl liked lookin' at him— watchin' him— even when Hank was doin' the most mundane shit, like right now, watchin' him doin' dishes. Nothin' fancy 'cept maybe the faded jeans that were kinda formed around his ass. They were a nice distraction. Then again just 'bout everythin' 'bout Hank was good for distraction. Earl's man was fifty years old and still had a boyish grin about him— kinda like Robert Redford— same hair and color eyes too. *Gawd, he was a lucky pecker. Why had he wasted so many years not being here with him hundred percent?*

Earl felt the stinging twitch in his nose like mustard seed and quickly dropped his head and his thoughts to the red-n-white checkered tablecloth. He scooted his hand forward and picked at a hole in it, lettin' the mindless poking sever what ached inside him. He'd sequestered himself over so many things through the years. Too many things he'd let eat at him while he kept silent, and he'd grown road-weary from it.

Earl looked up suddenly, twisting in his chair to glance over his shoulder out the window. The banged-up thing was still just quietly sittin' down at the dock, like some ghost waitin' for somethin' to happen. *But what?*

"So, what kinda plane is it anyways?" Earl called out behind him. He heard Hank movin' from the kitchen to the study. Maybe he hadn't heard him, or he was gonna go look it up. Hank was like that. Ever since he started writin'. He'd see somethin' on TV or somethin', and suddenly he was on the Google thing lookin' it up. Earl chuckled— *the shit Hank would find sometimes.*

The sound of somethin' dropping' on the table next to his arm roused him from his reflections, and Earl turned, seein' Hank had placed a book out, open to a page with a couple of planes pictured on the glossy paper. Hank tapped on one in particular.

"CF-AYO La Premier Norseman."

Earl grabbed up the book, glancing at the photo of the Royal Canadian Air Force Recovery Seaplane, then stared out the window. She was an exact match for the 1935 model plane. "So, what's she doin' here, Hank?"

Hank took the book from Earl's hands, folded it closed, and left it on the table, "I don't know, babes. I don't know much about things that vanish in thin air. I don't even believe in ghosts." He pulled on Earl's shoulder to urge him to turn and look at him. "Come watch TV with me. I'm missin' you." *Shit, he hadn't meant to say it quite like that.* The pursed-lips grin that was suddenly stamped on Earl's face said it weren't no kind thing for him to say. "I'm sorry. I just want to feel your arms around me."

Earl nodded at him and pushed up, stepping into his space. "You bet, babe." Earl's arms came around him and hugged him. "I'm in a need for some *Hankering* myself."

"I call little spoon."

"Wha— hey, now. How is it you're callin' little spoon already and—" he glanced at the clock, then back to Hank, "and we ain't even near bedtime yet."

Hank gave him a boyish grin and leaned in to deliver a mushy kiss. "I know. Just callin' in my reservations." He gave him another peck on the lips before heading off for the living room. Earl watched him like he was all proud and stuff and let out a huff. Seemed the weirdness was spreadin'. Even his lover was gettin' funny in the britches.

Earl went to the cupboard, grabbed the bag of chips, and followed after him, where they took their regular spots, stretching out together on the broken-in brown tweed couch. They had a quick haggling toss-up between *Castle* and *Sons of Anarchy*, and the loser got DVR'd for another time.

After some chuckles and droolin' over actor *Nathan Fillion*, what to watch next was usually a hotchpotch of channel- flippin'. To which, Hank had somehow managed to finagle control over the remote, on top of his earlier dibs on the little spoon spot.

"Hey— hey— hey, go back, go back." Earl's lumbering attention perked up at the mixed sounds of chainsaws and cheers.

Hank backtracked until they discovered *Lumberjack World Championship* reruns on ESPN. The television screen displaying four men on a stage with state-of-the-art high-powered chainsaws in a race to slice off disks from propped logs. *Two of the boys weren't bad on the eyes either.*

"Ha, you should find out about these things and put Wilson up there." Hank laughed, enjoyin' the high energy of the commentator as well as the crowd, as the boys on the TV competed to saw off four disks from their logs the fastest. The whole thing was over in little more than four or five seconds. Not bad at all.

Next up came a couple of gals on the chopping blocks.

"Put your knockers into it," Earl called out to cheer a heavyset contender on. "Att'ah girl!" He shouted when she managed to cleave her block in half after only a half a dozen chops into it, taking the win.

Hank was enjoyin' it just as much as Earl, but he couldn't help but take the occasional glance up at him to double-check his man wasn't lookin' out the window. He'd known it was gonna nag at Earl somethin' awful, but Hell fire, he didn't know what to do about it, either. They lucked out on the championships showing on TV, he guessed, with an energy and sport they could relate to. Even he did, though he'd worked in the mill as a latheman. Still, it was what they had both known most of their lives. He'd started off in a carpenter's workshop back home in Kentucky. But when he and Emma found out they had twins underway, bein' a shopkeeper for minimum wage wasn't gonna cut it. That's when

Uncle Willie had convinced him to come out here to the Poconos.

Hank twisted and glanced at Earl, seein' his man's eyes dance as he watched two returning champion climbers race for the top of a 250-foot pole. Hank didn't regret one damn thing in his life, 'cuz of it all, he'd landed right in Earl's arms.

"Well, I'll be damned," Earl muttered with a half grin.

"What?" Hank asked, turning back to the TV to see what had Earl surprised. The winning climber proudly held up his trophy overhead, and there was no missing it. The boy had a prosthetic arm.

"Say, how's Scottie anyway?" Right away Hank's thoughts went to one of the young men on Earl's crew who'd suffered a fate like the man on the TV.

"He's amazin'," Earl answered. "Kid don't let nothin' stop him. He's back on the crew even. It's hardly been a year and the docs said he was good to go. Them prosthetic guys made him a special arm with a custom hand that's molded to hook onto a chainsaw handle. He's out there right along with the rest of the guys like nothin' happened."

Hank smiled. That was awesome news to hear. Scottie was a good kid, been hangin' round since he was just a tot. Then one day when the crew was out loggin' up near the north state line, a steel rope line snapped. The boys scattered— Scottie barely managed to twist in time to keep from bein' cleaved in half. The braided cable severed his hand, and the chainsaw it was holdin' clean off. The docs gave him a choice: sew it back on and have only some limited use of it, or close his wrist up and get fitted with a prosthetic. For Scottie, half-ass wasn't a choice.

Hank was feelin' rather nostalgic suddenly about his relationship with Earl. Perhaps missin' out on their time last weekend did it, or maybe it was that seaplane out back. He wasn't sure, but he knew that what he was feelin' right now had nuttin' to do with TV, and everythin' to do with salt-n-pepper playgrounds. He kept up his tempting squirming until Earl's *Hankering* finally kicked in, and they were walkin' and undressin' their way to the bedroom.

Hank dropped down onto the bed, his hands groping over Earl's furry body before Earl could ease himself next to him. So distant tonight he seemed, and Hank wished to erase that from his man's mind.

Surely the plane wasn't the cause for all of this, right?

He slid his hand up Earl's body and around to his back to hug him, as Earl took hold of the back of his neck and pulled him in for slow tentative kissing. The moment seemed to pause right there, not stopping, but just kinda stuck on the kiss. It was odd from their normal Friday catch-up. Hank was mostly expectin' bear pawin' and stuff, seein' they'd missed a weekend together. But Earl's hands kept up around his head and shoulders, seemingly content to just kiss and nibble while Hank held him. Of course, Hank wasn't complainin', but it worried him some. Cuddling was good and fun and all, until someone got a hard on, which was him.

Just when Hank was thinkin' he may have to give his bear a kick to get him unstuck, Earl reached down, hooked Hank's leg, and hauled him over to sit straddled over his body as he rolled to his back.

"Mmmm, that's the Earl I was waitin' on." Hank groaned satisfactory for him.

"Oh, you was worried I wasn't gonna get my *Hankering* fix?"

Hank rolled his groin against Earl's cock, then bent over to nose him playful. "I might have started to worry you forgot in your absence."

Earl reached out for the nightstand, fumbled with a drawer, and fetched a bottle of lube. "I don't reckon that's ever gonna happen, babes."

"Good." Hank grinned into their kiss, taking the bottle from Earl. He poured a healthy dollop on his hand and started using it to coat both his and Earl's eager hard-ons together.

Earl tipped his head back and let out a pleasant sigh, palming his beefy hands up and down Hank's thighs, enjoying the hand job. Occasionally responding with a rise of his hips, lifting Hank in a slow urging hint to get him to move into a more accessible position.

Hank leaned forward, letting Earl's cock, already slicked up, to slip past his scrotum, then lowered back down, and rocked against the shaft slapping up against his crack.

Earl reached around him, both hands taking hold of Hank's ass cheeks, groping over them with a slow hunger, spreading them wide while his hips moved the tip of his blunt shaft over Hank's hole.

Hank's breath kicked up a slow notch, his body hungry to have his bear inside him. Still, he couldn't dispel the odd quietness or distance he felt comin' from Earl.

He wished nothin' more than to wipe all that away, if only he knew what it was, but he also knew Earl weren't much for talkin', and would stay as tight as a clam until he was ready. That's what thirty-seven years of being trapped in a marriage to Gracie had done to him. All Hank could do was love him right now.

"You want inside me, honeybear?"

"Ohhh— yeah, babe, let me inside you."

Hank sat up just as he felt his love's hand slip under him. He felt the blunt tip of Earl's cock sliding over his puckered entrance a couple of times, and then a heavy hand caught his hips, easing his body's weight to slowly become impaled. Hank hissed with the first sweet bite. He rocked his weight up and down, each micro-movement sliding farther and farther down. He was enjoyin' every bit of Earl's thickness as it stretched and filled his backside perfectly. There was somethin' to be thankful of, to find the one man you loved to be with— a curse when the fate of your life disagreed. It was a bonus for this ol' boy's dirty rotten mind when the cock he sat on had never ceased to stroke and stuff him so right.

Somethin' must have clicked, 'cuz what was slow easy in one moment was fed up with it in the next. Earl's hands tightened, putting a bit more weight into his pull. Hank, of course, obliged him and sank all the way down, lettin' out a drawn-out sigh. "Ahhh, honey." Hank rocked his ass, grinding into Earl's groin to seat that cock in him completely, and then the wave came, like ridin' a horse on an open field: no race for the end, but a might more than just a stride. His mountain man pushed up, meetin' his every downward stride to buck him right back up. Their bodies slapped in time, and their breaths bore the evidence of both the endurance and the pleasure. Growls and heavy breaths paired up like some erotic lullaby made to get a man hard, or in this case harder, 'cuz damn his dick was achin'. And as if Earl had heard Hank's thoughts and needs, one of those mountain-man hands let go of his hip, wrapped around his dick, and began to stroke him over somewhere between *too-fuckin'-maddenin'-slow* and *just-the-right-pace* to get him off in *zero-to-sixty* flat.

Hank dropped back some, his hand coming to land on Earl's thigh, and he held on while bucking up into Earl's fist. "Ohhh, shh-shit." He loved that fraction of time when it felt like his eyes rolled to the back of his head and his toes curled in mirror of his nuts. When everything coiled in and then suddenly exploded out in a jerkin', ground-rattling shockwave.

Hank heard Earl bite back his own growling pleasure that escaped in short grunts, and then Hank felt the hot wash of Earl's cum hitting his insides. He stilled his movements, not that he could move much with Earl's hands clamping down on his hips, locking him in place. "Oh, fuck yeah. That's always the best feelin'." Hank moaned out loud.

Feeling rather boneless after the wave was over, Hank let himself drop over on his side. The movement and angle had Earl's cock slipping out sooner then he wanted, but he was drained, and he didn't much care for long. Earl's head turned to look at him with a look that— well, it somehow told him he loved him. No smile, no words, but it was there clear as day in the darkness of their bedroom. He could see it in Earl's eyes, maybe some warm color in his cheeks added to it, and when Earl leaned over to kiss him, Hank felt it. *Always had.* No matter all the distance between them, he had always felt that.

Usually, they both dozed off after sex, but for some damn reason somethin' kept Hank up. The occasional thumb-strummin' of Earl's hand on his shoulder said he was awake too, and that wasn't good at all. Earl was good at shuttin' the world out, but he was also able to sleep like the dead most anytime. So, when somethin' was keepin' him awake, it was somethin' wrong. Hank was just waitin' for it to come out.

A fan in the window blew the cool mountain night air over their bodies, bringing with it the scent of rich greenery and a few flowering shrubs. The revolving blades added some pink noise to the otherwise quiet house. Hank was stretched out over Earl's chest with a leg tossed over his man's. His favorite position, he slept this way every Friday, Saturday, and Sunday. Only he weren't sleepin' right now.

"Hank?" Earl whispered in the darkness without stirring.

Hank remained still, almost frozen in place suddenly. It was one of those eerie silences that had the twists going on inside his stomach. He knew somethin' was goin' to come up, but he didn't want to know what it was, so he didn't ask, and he tried real hard to pretend he didn't feel it. But when Earl spoke his name in the dark room, Hank's insides seized up like an engine that just threw a rod. He forced himself to swallow, feelin' the fist, punchin' at the center of his chest, and the hard dry lump in his throat. "Yeah." His response croaked out.

"How come you've never asked me to leave her?"

Another swallow and Hank's lips twitched to form an answer. "'Cuz I know the grief you have to live with, and to force yourself to do so is hard enough. You don't need me naggin' you over what can't be done."

"Twenty-three years for you and me is a long time to endure this. And I decided it was time to stop."

Hank's head snapped up instantly with a horrified look. "Ya gonna leave me?"

Earl turned a bit, looking at him "No. No, never that." Earl took in a deep breath and let it out in a long sigh, and finally told him what he'd done. "I told Gracie I wasn't comin' back, and I was filin' for a divorce, like it or not."

Hank felt the small bit of fear drop, but he wasn't too quick to accept that everythin' was okay just yet. "But we talked about it. You said we needed another five years before—"

"Yeah, well— guess I went and done somethin' else, myself too." Earl let out another sigh and his gaze drifted up toward the ceiling, "I tell you, babe, one look at that baby girl and seein' the family all happy—" Earl shook his head, "and yet I couldn't be happy *with them* 'cause you weren't there *with me*."

3

Earl had the skillet going with piles of bacon and hash browns when Hank came in from the porch with his overnight bag in his hand.

"You forgot to bring this in." He waved it as he went by, toting it back to the bedroom.

"I was kinda preoccupied and all." Earl chuckled as he cracked open several eggs and tossed them into the same skillet. He hovered over for a moment, inhaling the aroma of good stuff, then grabbed a cookie sheet and laid it over top. He turned just as Hank returned from their room.

"What's this?" Hank held up a DVD of a kid's animation movie.

Earl let out another slight chuckle. "Oh, Nick and the kids stayed over for the weekend. Molly couldn't get out of work, so it was just him and the two boys, but they forced me to brush up on my movie knowledge."

"And I have to suffer 'cuz—?"

"'Cause it's funny. Trust me, you'll like it." Earl turned back to the stove, removed the cookie pan from the skillet, and began dicing up the breakfast conglomerate with a spatula. He grabbed a potholder, pulled the skillet from the stove, and served it up on the plates he already had waiting.

Breakfast would have been uneventful if Earl could just get himself to stop lookin' out the window, and of course every time he did, Hank would glance over his shoulder to see what got his attention, and of course it was that dern plane out there. Hank finally got fed up with it, dropped his fork on his plate, and put them damn southern elbows right on the table. *That's a big no-no down there for them south folk,* so he knew he was in trouble then.

"You look at that plane one more time and I'm gonna make you do some editin' for me."

Earl's head was instantaneously shaking side to side. "Um, hell no, I ain't doin' no editin'. I gotta mow the lawn on account it don't look like you did the whole time I was gone."

"'Cuz I knew you could do it when you got home."

"Well, that's a fine how-do-you-do," Earl grumbled. He shoveled the last morsel from his plate into his mouth, but he hadn't even gotten it chewed down when his eyes flickered back to the window again.

"Dammit to hell, Earl, that's it!" Hank snapped.

"How the hell am I not gonna look? Pray tell me—" Earl swept his arm up in grand announcement toward the window. Only when they both followed his thick arm out to where the subject of their indifference should have been floating— *nothin'.*

Earl felt the cheeks on his face droop clear off and he just stared a long silent moment. He didn't hear nothin'. Not a sound, no motorboat, no people, no plane engine. Nothin'— nada— zilch. So how the hell did it vanish? *For Christ's sake, it hadn't even been two minutes since he'd looked the last time.*

"Uh— ohh-kay, I think I'll go edit," Hank muttered.

Earl pushed up from the table, collecting their plates, keeping his head down as he did, so as not to be looking himself, not more than he cared too anyway. "I'll go mow."

That evening, Earl got the movie going just as Hank came in with a bowl of popcorn with extra melted cheese. Earl instantly grabbed a handful and stuffed the slimy kernels into his mouth, humming in satisfaction. He let out a funny little shimmy from his shoulders and leaned in to get a cheesy smooch off his man.

"You know we're gonna get fat one of these days if we keep eatin' this stuff." Earl plopped down on the tweed sofa, got his pillow perfect for movie watchin', and sat back to make space for Hank to lay against him.

"Yeah, well, then we'll just have to be two fat old guys who still love each other," Hank jeered happily as he chewed down a mouthful of their movie-night treat.

"Mm'kay," Earl hummed again as Hank stretched out, taking his place between Earl's legs with the bowl of cheese popcorn resting on his stomach. "Just makin' sure you know this, in case I don't stay perdy for long." Earl dropped his arms over Hank's chest, delivering a half hug to poke fun at Hank's southern drawl that, after all these years, still hung with him. But then the cheesy, sloppy goodness was beckoning him. Earl was too weak to resist, so he gave in and grabbed a handful of the popcorn concoction, then turned his focus to the TV as the movie started.

"Adventure is out there!" An animated child character's voice called out with enthusiasm. And thus began a montage of the movie's Mr. Fredricksen's life.

There was a reason he'd picked this one above all the others. Sure, *Finding Nemo* and that other one about the supersuits was pretty damned funny, but this one— about the boy growin' up with his best friend— how they got married with a dream and grew old together— and mostly how life got in the way of their dream to Paradise Falls— had hit Earl so hard, it hung in his soul and on his skin like melted cheese, only it didn't taste as good. Hoverin' like smog was more like it. All weekend with the kids it stuck on him. The more he noticed, the more he started to choke on it.

That Saturday mornin' when they'd all gone back to the hospital and his little Leanne handed over his first granddaughter. He'd looked into the baby-bundle's wee wittle eyes looking back up at him with a sleepy smile and he'd looked to see everyone else wearin' the biggest grandpop-smile only to see Gracie leerin' at him with so much hatred and loathin'.

It shouldn't have been that way; it should have been the face of the man he loved standing next to him. Earl's heart shattered that very moment. So much time had been lost lettin' life get in the way of his Paradise Falls. He'd nearly broke down just then in front of his daughter no less, too happy to give over his granddaughter just yet and too heartbroken that Hank wasn't with him to share in it— like he should'ah been.

He'd even walked over to the window, turning his back to the others, and cradled the tiny bundle against his face. He kissed her sweet pink head, and then used it to wipe the tears from his cheek.

Gracie got tired of waitin' her turn and started puttin' up a cussin'. She even pulled out the Lord's name in vain. Earl just shut her out, still lookin' out the window with his granddaughter and silently pointin' out to the mountains in the distance to where Hank could be found, wipin' another tear off with her fussy, little pink head. His grand babygirl was good to her ol' grandpop that way.

Behind him, the cussing continued. To Earl it was just another sound that separated him from them while he drowned on the inside. He couldn't count the times he'd heard it 'cause he did his best not to. Didn't matter where they were either, he never answered Gracie's rants, and he never shouted back at her. Just like that day at the hospital, he let Gracie continue on until Leanne snapped about the GD word.

Earl'd said nothing. He never did. No matter what Gracie threw at him, he had learned a long time ago, he couldn't shut her up, so— he shut her out.

It kept her from makin' him the bad guy in the eyes of their kids, 'cause he never once raised his voice at her, let alone his hand. Not since the night after she'd found out about him givin' Hank all his inheritance. He and Gracie fought 'til the walls of Jericho rumbled over that, each of them givin' out their ultimatums, and what would happen if the other pulled him out of the closet for all of Scranton and the Poconos to know.

The movie weren't but about ten or so minutes into it when the boy, now an old man, led his wife up a hill to surprise her with a picnic, and a planned trip to finally get to their *Paradise Falls*. Only the Mrs. Fredrickson collapsed on that hill, and then shortly after— she passed away. Nothin' left but the old man and his grief of things not done.

Earl tried his damnedest not to let it get to him again, but he wasn't winnin' on it. *Stupid movie.* He felt the tingling in his face, and the moment he felt the slight quiver in his lips, he knew he'd already failed. The small sniffle was all it took, and Hank was sittin' up to look at him. Surely, he'd say somethin' smart-alecky about cryin' over a kid's film and then Earl'd be able to shake-off the emotions that were hurtin' so hard inside, but Hank saw what

Earl wanted to hide. Hank knew there weren't no jokes to be made about it.

"Earl— what's happened you're not tellin' me?"

Earl threw an elbow up on the sofa back and proceeded to chew on his fingers a moment. He shook his head like there weren't an answer to give. Only there was, he just weren't no good at turnin' all that bottled-up shit into words.

❧

Hank could count on his hand all the times he'd seen Earl get worked up and emotional. His lover had gotten so used to shuttin' everythin' out and lockin' himself away, yet when they were together Hank could see the relief in him. Earl didn't bring his hate up here, or his anger or unsettlement. *Here* was like a holiday, his getaway, free to let his johnny boys hang loose, and just be himself. So, when Earl was an open book with his emotions, it meant there was too much to bottle up any more and somethin' in his life needed to change.

"Talk to me. Let me know where ya are."

"We've missed so many things." Earl's voice nearly cracked trying to answer. And glistening pools of tears flooded his big brown eyes.

A tear broke loose and came down the size of a river falling down his cheek, vanishing into the scrubby beard. The sight of it broke Hank's heart, and he wanted to chase after it, keep it close to him, like it was somethin' he had to protect with his life.

Earl didn't even seem to realize it had happened. His head still moved side to side before settling on his fingers again when the next thought came out. "All on account of her. But the kids—"

Hank shook his head, and he reached out, resting his hand on Earl's thigh. "Then you can't do this. Don't give them up for me. I'm not goin' nowhere. If this is all the life we get, then it's the best damn life we have. And I ain't gonna complain about it."

"No." Earl took Hank's head in his hands and held him a moment, making him see him. "I've made you wait long enough. I've waited long enough. It's time for life to be about *us*— together— always."

"But—"

"No buts. When I leave here, somewhere down the side of that mountain I pass through somethin'. Like a car warsh that strips every part of me bone-dry. Every color and emotion. Nothin' but an empty tin can gettin' pushed 'round to make an appearance until it's time to come back." Earl tugged Hank into him until their heads touched, and he spoke as if in prayer. "I want to watch my grandkids grow up, but not if it means I can't be me anymore, and not if it means givin' up another moment to share all of it with you."

Despite the awkward angle, Hank was wrapped around Earl in a bear hug that was gonna last for days— he could just tell. He had lost his two boys down one side of these mountains, and he would never have grandkids. So, it broke his heart to hear Earl say anythin' along the lines that might cost him the pleasure of seein' his own grow up. But havin' him here, with him from now on, healed that same heart. So, he wasn't gonna complain on this one either. "You get little spoon tonight," Hank mumbled into his man's neck.

4

"Daddy, what is all this crazy nonsense Mom is goin' on about?" Earl's daughter and youngest of the kids was harpin' at him over the phone. Good thing she didn't sound anythin' like her momma.

"Baby-girl, it was just time I set myself free and be happy with the person who has always made me happy."

"I'm not talkin' about that. I'm talkin' about you and Hank not comin' down for Crystal's christenin'."

Earl thought for sure his stomach had just fell right out and splattered over the floor. He had been preparin' himself for the whiplash the kids were likely to throw at him after Gracie had her chance to fill their ears with her version of their morbid marriage life. What he didn't expect was what sounded like acceptance. "Leanne, what you askin'?" He had to ask it just to be sure.

"Mom said you are turnin' your back and leavin' all of us just to be with Hank. That you hate us, and you refuse to come down for your granddaughter's christenin'!"

Earl could hear it in her voice; she was nearly in tears over the news as she rambled over the phone line.

"No. I would never give you kids up. I just had to give Gracie up, baby-girl."

The line went quiet a moment. *"So, Uncle Hank isn't really—?"*

"No, he isn't," Earl went ahead and answered. He had waited, prepared, and even recited what his response would be to every question that might possibly be asked. He only hoped that no matter how painful it was, he would be allowed to answer them, 'cause the alternative meant his kids hated him as much as Gracie did and didn't care what his answer was.

"S-so how long?"

He could hear the hurt, but if she was willin' to be strong enough to ask, he was goin' to be honest enough to answer. "Twenty-three years."

"But you still love us, too, right?"

"Of course, and I always will, Leanne. You kids were the only reason your momma and I stayed together."

"Somehow, I'm bettin' them chains were a slightly different size than you're tellin', but if you're not wantin' to tell me, that's okay. Hearin' mom's side was bad enough. What is important is you're goin' to be here."

Earl kept silent; part of his vow was that he wasn't gonna do anythin' without Hank there with him to share in it.

"You and Hank— together." She added. And that was it, his heart fell out and landed right next to his stomach. A few tears cropped up somehow, and he was wishin' he had a little pink baby head to wipe them off with. *Little baby Crystal was good at doin' that for her ol' grandpop.*

That was two days ago. Now he was standin' in the mirror fussin' with the tie Hank had picked out for him, along with the new suit. New, on account the last time he wore one was for his folks' funeral, and for some reason, it shrank over the years. So, they had to go out and buy a new one. Hopefully this one was shrink resistant, since he had no clue when he'd have to wear it again.

After he'd gotten all suited up, Earl felt the walls closin' in on him, and he was startin' to cook in his suit already. So, he went out to sit on the stoop while he waited for Hank to finish gettin' ready. He sat there starin' at the plane. He scratched at the scrub on his jaw, wondering what the hell he was supposed to think about the plane.

Well—

Well, he didn't rightly know what to think. After all, what does one normally think when a twenty-six-foot-somethin' long and just-as-wide-on-her-wingspan airplane shows up like she fell from the trees and then the next second vanish like she never was? Yet, sure as shit, there she was sittin' back at the dock just as ugly and perdy as she damn well pleased, making a mockery of his and Hank's heads.

Earl switched from beard scratching to tugging at his ear a moment. Scranton had a library, but he didn't reckon they'd have much on ghost planes there. His ponderings were put on hold when Hank showed up at his side, all dressed up and ready to go. Earl pushed up, drawin' in a deep breath, and catchin' a nice whiff of Hank's cologne and hopefully some courage and endurance along with it, as he looked his lover and life partner over. "Dayyum. I oughta get you to wear suits more often."

Hank grinned wide for him. "Yeah? And how long you reckon I'd wear it for?"

"Not long." Earl pursed his lips in a frumpy smile, then turned, throwing his elbow out in offering. "Shall we?"

Hank gave a nervous smile, but took his arm all the same, and they headed for the truck.

"Hell's fire. I'm sweatin' bullets already and we ain't even gotten on the road yet," Hank muttered, climbin' into the passenger side.

"It's the suit." Earl gave him an excusable nod. "The suits are hot."

As they drove down towards town, Earl couldn't shake the storm of emotions rumblin' through him. They were like a thunderstorm trapped just on the other side of the mountain ridge. There was even a few times Earl forgot to get a move on after stoppin' at a stop sign, and again at a light not realizing it'd done turned green some time ago.

Hank had offered to drive, and while he appreciated the offer, Earl had it in his head he had to do this himself. All these years drivin' back to the life that was his prison, this time he had to face the wrath of his furlough. It was a bittersweet freedom.

When they got to the church, they both just kinda sat there— idle— *stallin'*, if he had to be truthful about it.

They only seemed to move in increments. First, it was them just sittin' in the truck, starin' at the building as if somethin' miraculous would happen and then they could all just go on home. They went through it again, pausing at the steps before the door. Doors that were closed 'cause they were late.

Like so many other folks, Earl was a God-lovin', believing' man, but the number of times he'd gone to church could be summed up rather quickly with little more purpose than the holiday sermon, a few weddings and deaths, and now a grandbaby blessing could be added among them.

For some reason, as Earl reached for the door, he wanted to make a joke along the lines of *"watch me part the crowd like Moses and the Red Sea"*. But glancin' at Hank, who was sufferin' a case of the flop sweats and lookin' a little pinkered, had Earl choosin' otherwise, and quietly they went in.

Earl couldn't tell if the uneasiness in the air was 'cause everyone knew or 'cause he had it in his mind that they did. Either way, he was wound up so tight inside, one noise— one clatterin' sound of somethin' fallin' to the floor— and Earl was gonna have a heart attack. *Shell shock*— yeah, that about summed it up— and he felt like he was sufferin' a severe case of it. He'd give anythin' to trade up with Hank right now. A severe case of the flop sweats seemed like vacation time to what he was feelin'.

Thankfully there was one comfort: when in church, even the worst of Christians tend to behave themselves. And good thing too, 'cause seein' the relief and gratitude that lit up his daughter's face when she saw him come in was a welcomin' he surely needed. However, when she gleefully waved at him and Hank, Earl's heart jammed up where his throat was. He was struck down with a sudden case of the cold sweats followed with a tad of stage-fright horrors when half the church turned to see who had brightened Leanne Knox-Munro's face like that.

Earl swallowed hard and quickly slid into a pew, pulling Hank along with him. Not 'til he was already sitting down did he realize he'd landed next to Ol' Thomas Kennedy, their local sheriff. Yep, the very same one whose daughter was married to Earl's second oldest son, Nick.

Earl took a deep breath and let it all blow out in his own version of a duck-bill expression. *It was gonna be a long two hours.*

Funny how religion and hate go hand in hand sometimes, as if being religious gave a person the badge of honor to express their hatred without accountability, 'cause sure as shit will stink in the yard, the first step outside after the services, words were said. And those sayin' them made damn sure they were loud enough so Earl heard them all.

"You got some nerve showin' your face 'round here, Earl." One in particular spoke up. Doing so from a safe distance just in case Earl would do something completely out of character, like turn radically violent and maybe punch the man. The idea may have even slipped across Earl's mind. But then he saw the judgment came from his neighbor, Carl Gibbons.

Earl scratched over his beard a moment. He and Carl had been neighbors going on for some thirty years now. They had waved to each other nearly every day as they got home from work and watched out for each other's kids. In fact, when Carl had a stroke while mowin' his lawn a few years back, it was Earl who'd found him, and rushed him to the hospital. Now— in the blink of an eye and one spoken word that forever would identify him as different from all of them— all that seemed to change. The moment Earl was gay, he became insignificant to the man's memories or opinion of what kind of man Earl still was.

"Sorry to hear you say that, Carl," Earl finally answered and headed down the steps. He could tell his welcome at the church right now was a fragile one. And this day wasn't about him; it was about Leanne, her husband, David, and Earl's grandbaby. The rest would be dealt with in increments, better saved for grocery-store and post-office errands, not Crystal's christening.

A firm hand slapped Earl on the shoulder, and he glanced up as Thomas strolled by a stride faster than he had been. Thomas gave Earl a nod and placed his Stetson on his head. "It was a good service today." He nodded once more and continued down the walkway.

Carl apparently didn't see it that way and followed after Earl and Hank to sling a few more insults at him. *That*, to Earl, was chasin', and it set him on edge, more so than he already was. Scranton was a small town, and everyone knows small towns have a tendency to turn into mobs once one person picks up the pitchfork and sets a bonfire on a subject.

"You should be ashamed of yourself, desecratin' a church with your presence!" Carl shouted out, coming up behind them.

Earl stopped, coming about to face his accuser. Carl jumped back once more, the movement perhaps annoying Earl more than the words. Earl had never been a violent man. "Now why you gotta go sayin' some shit like that, huh?"

"God hates queers, and he don't want them in his house."

Earl just shook his head. *Funny how you can live next to a man for a lifetime and never know him.* "Carl, I don't know what kind of God you believe in, but my Lord and Savior isn't that weak. There is absolutely nothin' I can do in my life that has power over him to desecrate anythin' of his or do anythin' that he doesn't want me to do." Earl thought for sure that would be the end of it. Then again, Earl had been known to be wrong about some things from time to time before. Well, it turned out he was dead wrong about this one. He and Hank had just reached the curb when Carl had managed to build up enough cowardly courage to say one more thing.

"And to think all this time I lived next to you, puttin' my kids at risk of bein' raped by a perverted pedophile queer!"

Okay, so Earl wasn't a violent man, and he usually could get around any argument or fight without it comin' to blows, but not this time. Carl couldn't jump back fast enough before Earl sent him to the ground with one solid connection of his sledgehammer-sized fist— lights out in one punch.

The mayhem followed, as that mob mentality reared up its ugly head, with Gracie stokin' the fires from the sidelines.

Leanne started shouting and crying for everyone to shut up. David did what he could to restore peace for his wife's sake. Earl's boys Owen, Nick, and Mason were next to step in. Whatever hurtin' they had of their own, they weren't gonna stand by and let anyone insult their pop none, as Carl had just done. Earl and Hank saw each other as if in the tunnel of a windstorm. It was happenin' whether they contributed to it or not, and there weren't no stoppin' it yet. It had to run its course. They both glanced at the truck, thinkin' to just get in, and leave the rest to fight it out, but that was when someone threw a punch at Mason.

Mason wasn't the type to back down either; almost a mirror of a younger Earl, he ploughed Tyron Walker into the sidewalk for it. The shouting now took on a different tone, and the women cried out to have the fight stopped. Their pastor called for peace with reminders that they were all still on church property.

Thomas had stopped his truck and got back out, watching, hovering on the fence, as to either, staying back as a family member or engaging as sheriff. He glanced Earl's way, a silent warning that he'd have to take Mason in if he did get involved. Earl waved Hank in for backup and finally managed to haul his son, Mason, off his best friend. Mutual friends of the boys moved in and shuffled Mason back inside the church, Tyron took off in another direction, both boys sporting the starters cf some black eyes and battle wounds.

The rest of the guests broke off in tearful disapproving groups, distancing themselves from Hank and Earl, or just getting in their cars and going home.

Nick shuffled his family into their van and sped off, and Mason managed to slip out the back to avoid getting into another fistfight with anyone over the *queer* word. While the kids had not shared in the name-throwing at their pop, their pain and bewilderment was evident when both left without a kind word to him either. The riff cut into Earl deeply.

Earl had known— or rather he feared— this would happen. Perhaps he had been wrong; maybe he should have told them long ago.

He shook his head at all that had transpired today. Just more of the *could'ah— should'ah— would'ah—* those damn things you look back on now, but you knew damn well you didn't see them comin' at the time. So, there weren't nothin' to do about it, though that didn't stop the regrets from cavin' in on him.

Earl reached back, his hand catching Hank's and instantly locking their fingers. He needed the *rootage* right here, right now, 'cause he weren't too sure this big ol' tree was gonna manage to weather the storm this time. Hank stood strong at his side, just like Earl knew he would, as they watched his family unravel. The dam had broken; now all was left was the effects of the wash out. He only hoped his kids would let him rebuild with them, a new life that included Hank as his husband, not best friend, *sans uncle.*

Leanne was over alongside of the hedge that bordered the churchyard. Their baby was turned over to Leanne's closest friend while David did all he could to console his wife as she bawled her little eyes out over all the fightin' that had transpired all on account of him, who he was and what *they* thought that meant.

"Pop?"

Earl turned, seeing his oldest, Owen, coming up cautiously. It was clear he was troubled by the news and mayhem that had followed in its wake. Bad enough the boy grew up feelin' like he was a mismatch for the family, only now to be told in the worst kinda way his pop was gay.

Hank pulled his hand free and patted Earl's shoulder. "I'll be in the truck," He whispered, then stepped away to give Owen the space he needed to talk with his pop.

Earl could see the question all over Owen's face, and he nodded, lettin' him know it was true, but everythin' would be okay. Only Earl didn't dare try to reach out for him just yet. Owen, even as a grown man, had always been a bit on the skittish side. Unlike his mother, Earl had learned to give Owen his space and let him come to him when he was good and ready. Earl, however, also knew how to stay close by, so his son didn't have to look far when he was. "It's okay, son. It's not anythin' new for me. Just lettin' it be known, only I would've rather told you kids another way."

"So why didn't you?"

Earl's lips rolled over a moment to hide the fact he had to bite his tongue for what he wanted to say about their mother. "'Cause as long as I kept quiet about it, so did your momma. And that was a good thing."

Owen took a step closer, at least enough of one that they were no longer lookin' like they were purposely keepin' a distance in case bein' gay was contagious. "I— I don't know what to think about all this just yet. I mean, I guess it shouldn't have come as such a surprise, seein' you were always with Unc— with Hank." Owen made the quick correction. "But I just kept tellin' myself it was because Mom was always such a bitch to you."

"Owen!" Gracie was calling for him from behind, and they both looked to see her coming across the parking lot. She had that fretful look about her, like her world was crumblin' at her feet and she was the damsel in distress. Now she was determined to collect the kids so she could make them see she was right about everything. To keep them on her side.

"Not now, Mom! I need to talk to Pop a bit." He shouted over his shoulder at her, probably hopin' she wouldn't try to interrupt as she always did.

"Owen, honey, he ain't even your real pop."

Earl couldn't believe he'd heard her say it. Every siren and red light went off like an air raid in him. "Gracie, you shut the fuck up, right here and now! Don't you dare say another word to him!" He bellowed out, but already Owen was turning with a disbelieving look at her.

"What did you just say?" Owen gasped.

Gracie glared at Earl, the anger in her eyes sayin' she had every intention of keepin' up the fight. She was far from bein' exhausted by it, and she turned her attention back to their son. She was out to hurt Earl, and she wasn't even seein' how she was gonna hurt their son in the process. Gracie was blinded with her hate for him, and that's all she saw. "Owen. Earl Knox—"

"Gracie, I mean it!" With the intent of usin' every bit of his size and lumberjack bear to threaten her down, Earl stepped directly into her path, blockin' her from his son. "Don't you dare do this to him! I mean it!"

"And you knew this?" A meek question was asked behind him, silencin' them both.

Earl's heart cracked. All his life with Gracie had been hell, but dammit he loved his fuckin' kids. Gracie was goin' to see him to his grave, either without his Hank or without his kids. And that just weren't gonna do. His face drew up in an overbearing scowl as he stood over Gracie. "You're not takin' my kids away from me and that's that." He bit the words out, and then turned to look at his eldest son; the worry lines that came from the genes of another melted Earl's walls. "All I know, and have ever known, is the day you was born, I loved you. And there isn't been a time in my life that I didn't."

Whatever Owen was thinkin' or feelin', Earl couldn't see the first clue about it. His boy'd grown up to be just like his pop, with an unwaverin' ability to hide away his emotions. *Dammit.* Earl wished it was the one thing Owen and the other boys didn't take after, but then what else was they gonna get from him after all these years of hidin' himself from Gracie's hate? And then it happened.

Owen teetered on his feet. Earl reached out and snatched him, pulling him in for a hug.

Owen clamped onto him.

"It's okay, son. I gotcha," Earl whispered to him. "Always have."

He felt Owen noddin' into his chest, lettin' Earl know
he knew that.

5

Two weeks seemed to drag by. Earl took a leave of absence from work to give himself, as well as everyone else, some time to calm down over the shocking news. At least Gracie's version of it anyways. Earl hadn't even bothered go down to the house to claim any of his things. Though Leanne had called to say she, Owen, and Mason had gone over to gather them when their momma threatened to have a backyard roast. David had purchased one of them storage units with the promise it'd all be there when he was ready. Other calls included Gracie's lawyer, but there weren't no surprises there either. One surprise he did get, however, was from his bosses. It seemed they weren't keen on losin' him, regardless of what others thought. Despite some egos, loggin' wasn't done with their peckers, so where Earl put his weren't no concern of theirs. But they did offer him a fresh start if he wanted it.

A new contract was comin' in with a new crew. Earl'd already been among the few being considered to get it; now, he was gettin' first dibs if he wanted it.

"I need a word for needy," Hank called out over his laptop, puttin' his *focused* time into his writing out on the porch that afternoon.

"Needy is a good word," Earl joked, recallin' a line from a favorite movie, as he read his newspaper.

"I already used that one though."

Earl glanced over at him. "They got rules about not usin' the same word more than once?" He made no remorse that he was badgerin' his mate.

Hank was most likely about to give him one of those long theoretical reasonin's them authors have for everythin' when they heard the crunch of gravel under tires comin' down the driveway. Earl hopped up to his feet to go see who was comin' unannounced, but he came to a stop outside and stared down toward the lake. *Damned thing was gone again.*

Hank nearly slammed into Earl at the bottom of the step, not plannin' he would come to such an abrupt stop. One look over Earl's shoulder and it was self-explanatory. Well, not that either of them could actually 'splain it. He'd been readin' up on ghost ships and the sort ever since it'd done the first magic trick. Most tied into tales about the Bermuda triangle, but there weren't nothin' like that 'round here. Hell's fire, they didn't even have a single UFO story 'round these parts.

He heard the car stop at the bottom of the drive and honk the horn. "Must be our cue." Hank slapped Earl on the shoulder and pushed him to get goin' again.

Turned out to be a surprise visit from Earl's daughter, Leanne.

"Baby-girl? What'cha doing here? Everythin' alright?" Earl spilled with a slew of questions as they caught up to the car.

Leanne was digging in the backseat for something and suddenly popped her head out. "Y'all forget your manners or somethin'?"

Hank glanced at Earl, who gave him the same clueless look accentuated with one of those four-finger beard-scratchin' jobs.

"Some help over here?" She added as she pulled her baby from the car seat. She shot them both a look and shook her head at them. "Baby gear?" Her pitch went up with the sassy revelation that travelin' with babies did indeed require a considerable amount of it.

"Oh." Hank grinned. He still wasn't too sure what was goin' on. For one, the kids hadn't been up to the house in years and usually only when Earl brought them up. "Best hop to it then, huh?" He joked, seein' as Earl apparently didn't have a clue either. It was best to just go with the flow and all.

Leanne hit the button on her key-bob-remote-thingy and the hatchback floated up. There in the back was a pile of the *said mentioned* baby gear, includin' a box of goodies from the town's farmer's market. Once more Hank and Earl exchanged looks as they loaded up their arms and hauled in more stuff than even a newborn baby was gonna need for a day. However, as the realization set in, the deep, goofy grins took permanent residence on their faces. Leanne had brought Earl's grandbaby up for some one-on-one, and Hank was gonna get to be a part of it.

Guess he wasn't gonna get no writin' done today after all, Hank thought, but he was alright with that, as he hauled two bags, plus some long rectangular thingamajig that he didn't recognize, inside.

With the overhaul of stuff inside, Hank and Earl came out on the porch, where Earl right away relieved Leanne of her own burden and started up blowin' raspberries. Hank moved in for a hug from Leanne, then saddled up behind Earl to watch Crystal's face light up with wide-eyed surprise from her grandpop's attention. That and maybe the tickling beard, too.

"Whew, what a drive." Leanne sat down in the swing at the end of the porch and began to chatter away about her drive up as she pulled her long hair up over her head and fanned herself a moment. "I am so glad Crystal slept the whole way. I'd forgotten how much of a drive this is. The scenery is so beautiful, but I swear those slopes scare the dickens out of me."

"Not that I am complainin', baby-girl, but what brings you up anyways?" Earl asked, droppin' down in the wicker love seat against the house catty-corner from the swing. He scooted over so Hank had some room to join him.

Before Hank could take the offered prime spot, worry lines appeared on Leanne's forehead, and pursed lips tried to hide the quiver there, stilling Hank's feet.

Leanne raised her chin, pretendin' she could be strong. *God bless her little heart but she was precious.* "Lee, honey? What's happened?" Hank said as he sat down next to her instead. That's when she flung her arms around him and started cryin'.

"Oh, Uncle Hank it's awful. The things some of them are sayin'." The words were muffled by his shoulder.

Hank held on tight with no intentions of lettin' go. He brushed over her back with his hands to calm her down, but she only cried more. He watched Earl. The pain clouded over his eyes as he snuggled into his granddaughter, but while Hank could see his man's pain, what he didn't see was regret. Earl refused to regret lettin' anyone know they were together, and it was goin' to stay that way. Still, Hank couldn't help but hurt that Earl had given up so much. He had endured so much over these years only to have it come to this.

Leanne's snifflin' drew quiet, and she pushed off, wipin' her nose with the back of her hand. Hank patted at his pockets, found his handkerchief, and handed it to her.

"Anyways—" she started, blowing her nose into the old-school offering, then looked up at him and then to Earl. "Nick and Molly were over, and they started arguin' about whether or not they would let the boys see you again. Daddy, I got so mad at them." She choked on the sob that threatened to start up again. "How dare they? Molly said she didn't want you over at their house on account of she didn't want the neighbors thinkin' they were gay or supportive of gays and all. Nick said he was likely just gonna go along with it because he was tired of arguin' with her about it. But that's not even right. Molly's daddy is your best friend and even he didn't care." She blew her nose once more and leaned against Hank.

He tucked her head under his chin, and rubbed her arm, keeping her hugged tight into him.

"David came home from work the other day. Said some of the guys at the mill have been chewin' the cud about it as well. Scottie got sent home after punchin' one of the guys out for somethin' he said." She sputtered out a half laugh, "David said Scottie hit Leon so hard he nearly sent him flyin' across the room."

"Punchin' one another out isn't goin' to help folks accept this."

"Then what will?" Leanne turned to look at her daddy.

Hank looked too, 'cuz Earl was his strength, and right now he kinda needed a little of it.

"By not lettin' any of it change me and Hank. Life will be what it is. Sure, some friends will be lost, but I am not gonna sacrifice another day with him for them. I've done enough of that." Earl pulled his granddaughter in for a snuggle, kissing the top of her head. "I need him in my life more than I need those other people, baby-girl."

"But where does that leave us?"

"Oh, baby-girl. I love you kids with everythin' in me, but I am hollow if Hank can't be with me to share my joy of watchin' you kids go through life."

More tears spilled down her cheeks, but this time she smiled, too.

Hank was sure he felt some dust gettin' in his eyes just then, and he could've sworn he saw Earl scrub his face over his granddaughter's head. "Come on. What'da ya say we go in and have some lunch?" Hank offered, thinkin' a change of subject was needed.

Earl perked up at the suggestion. Lunch sure did sound good, but when his eyes went to the water, Hank caught it.

They'd nearly forgotten about their plane. Inside was the better part of the idea, 'cuz this just wasn't the right time to try goin' and 'splainin' what couldn't be 'splained anyways. That idea got even better than better when Earl passed Crystal over to him to hold while he went in to make the lunch.

It's one thing to be lookin' at a tiny bundle of bobbing-head and arms and legs that curled and kicked without any true motor control; quite another when the little bundle was in his hands and stealing some prime real estate in his heart. *Damn dust and stuff was really getting in the way of his eyesight just then.* Crystal blinked her deep blue eyes up at him and her tiny whisper of eyebrows went up in surprise. That's when Hank went through a sudden attack of goofy-face syndrome. The bundle in his arms responded with high-pitched squeals and bubbles which translated to *all good-stuffs* in baby talk— until she spit up on him.

After lunch for them and a bottle for Crystal, followed up with her throwing up on Hank, Leanne put her daughter down in the rectangular thingamajig that had miraculously unfolded into a travel crib, now takin' up the center of the living room.

"So how 'bout a swim while she naps?" Leanne asked, coming back to the kitchen just as they were finishing with putting up the dishes, and pulling a roast out to start thawing for later.

Hank shot a glance at Earl, panicking for an excuse.

"Uh, we— we can't," Earl stammered.

"Why not? Come on, I could really use a cool down."

"Well— becaaaaaause—" Earl looked at Hank for a substitute excuse to not go down to the dock, drawin' blanks of his own.

"'Cuz— shit—" Hank stalled, tryin' to think of somethin'. He shook his head at Earl 'cuz he didn't have one.

"Ssssssnakes!" Earl finally fished out a makeshift cover-up.

Hank snapped around to face Leanne, takin' the answer and runnin' with it. "Yes. Snakes. We have snakes."

"Oh, and terrible snakes, too," Earl added, shakin' his head to indicate swimmin' was out of the question.

"So don't you have a shotgun handy for that?"

"But these are big ones," Hank stammered.

"Y'all are crazy." She looked from Hank to her daddy and back again. She was clearly seein' right through them and knews they were up to somethin'. "Fine, you two can stay here and watch Crystal. I'm goin' for a swim."

Earl's hands went up in the air as if to stop her, but he quickly corrected his movement and brushed his hair back instead.

Hank had no idea he'd done relatively the same thing until Leanne's eyes went first to Earl's hands that were now landing on top of his head then looked to his own. "What? My head itched." Hank made excuses for some dumb reason, then looked away as if that would erase the fact he just made them both look very guilty of somethin'.

"Y'all really don't want me goin' down there, do you?"

"Baby-girl, the truth is, Hank and I was kinda foolin' around down on the dock earlier and we uh— we may have left a few things down there."

Leanne's face went red instantly and her eyes grew wide. "Ummm— yeah, that was more information than I needed, Daddy." She was the one scratchin' at her head this time, clearly embarrassed by the suggestion that her pop might possibly have *sex* like other adults do.

Funny how that always seemed to gross a kid out, but where do they think kids came from if'n it weren't for sex? Well maybe not from gay sex, but still funny.

"Okay, so maybe we can just watch TV then or somethin'."

"Good idea," Hank and Earl both blurted out in unison, and the three of them piled into the family room to talk and watch TV. Hank pulled out his laptop to write some and that led to Leanne askin' questions about what he wrote. That, of course lead to more red faces, and she stopped askin' for specifics.

When Crystal woke they all went for a walk along the trails. They returned in time for supper, and then gathered once more in the family room.

❧

Leanne sat on the sofa watchin' as her daddy and Uncle Hank played on the floor, takin' turns givin' her daughter raspberries on her cheeks and belly. Crystal squealed with delight each time.

Leanne watched as the two exchanged glances with each other. How their faces lit up with happiness, not only for havin' the time with their granddaughter, but to be able to share the moment. She couldn't recall a single time in her life that her daddy looked happier. He loved them and that had always shown on his face, but it was rarely expressed openly, as if somethin' around him kept him suppressed all these years.

She felt a swelling ache in her heart suddenly that soon had her bawling. Mom had been wrong. Daddy hadn't gone gay because he hated his family. Gay didn't mean he didn't want to be with them either.

He just wanted to be with Hank and not their mom. *Here*, he was happy. *Together*, they were happy, and they were takin' advantage of sharin' Crystal as if it might be the only moment they could have her together. They were like two babblin' fools. There was no evil here at all, just love—and a lot of it.

"Daddy, I love you!" She blurted aloud suddenly. Her daddy and Hank both suddenly rolled up to look at her. Worry lines creased their faces, and Earl tucked Crystal into a hug against his shoulder to keep her comfy while he looked at Leanne.

"Baby-girl, what's wrong?"

More tears poured out of Leanne's eyes, and she smiled, shaking her head. "Nothin' is wrong. Not a thing. I just love you and I want you to know mom's wrong. You don't hate us, you just love Hank, too, because he makes you happy where mom couldn't. And I want you to know I don't want my daughter growin' up without both her grandpops in her life. Only, I want her to know you as who you really are. No secrets from her, okay?"

Hank just sat there lookin' all stupefied. Earl practically fell back on his heels, once everythin' his daughter said set in. His baby-girl loved him, even knowin' he was gay, and his granddaughter would grow up knowin' that.

Hank couldn't hold it in any longer and he wrapped himself around Earl, kissin' him and the little bundle of pink joy between them. They exchanged an innocent kiss, then they both kissed their granddaughter at the same time, which got interrupted with an ear-piercin' squeal.

A moment later, Earl returned to his back on the floor with Crystal takin' flying lessons on outstretched arms as she was passed from one grandpop to the next. "Do ya hear that, precious? You get to grow up with both grandpops."

"Pawpaw," Hank instantly corrected him as he got to take his turn holdin' her. "He just didn't say it right," Hank told his new granddaughter proudly.

Earl took a double take at Hank. "Good gawd, you are truly southern."

"I am." Hank beamed and brought his squealin' granddaughter down for a raspberry on her belly, which was welcomed with more bubbles, and another one of her signature high-quality squeals.

"This calls for ice cream," Leanne announced, hopping off the couch, and heading for the kitchen.

"I second that." Hank got up to join her, as well as to go pull out the *for-special-occasions* Rocky Road Double Fudge he kept hidden from Earl, just to be sure they didn't get too fat too quickly in their old age.

Leanne grabbed bowls and searched the cupboards for toppings, playfully doin' a happy dance when she discovered mini-marshmallows and fudge sauce. "So, you gonna join me in a sugar coma, Daddy-Hank?"

Hank stopped mid-scoop and looked at her.

When she realized he hadn't answered, she turned to find a blank face on him. "I'm sorry. Was that wrong?" She asked apologetically.

"N-no. Not at all. It's just—" he grinned softly, "it's been a long time since I heard someone call me daddy."

Leanne looked down in sudden remorse. "Oh, Hank, I'm sorry, I didn't mean—"

"No, it's okay." He quickly grabbed her and pulled her in for a hug. "It felt good actually."

Leanne pushed against him; leaning her head back to see in his face, just to be sure, and when he nodded to her with teary blue eyes that it really was okay, she flung her arms around his neck, where she stayed for a long time. Hank was just fine with that, too.

Evening was drawing late on them, and it was time for Leanne to head on back to town. They'd held out to the last moment enough. But at least they'd gotten to spend time with their grandbaby together and knew there would be more of that to come. They'd also shared that moment *together*.

Hank and Earl watched the new mommy pack up all the modern gadgets of baby gear like a pro, and they hauled it all back to the car, sans the farmer's market goodies. Those miraculously managed to stay inside the house.

Leanne crawled back out of the car for final good-byes after she got her daughter installed— strapped— ratcheted— and super glued into the modern technological wonder of a baby seat that had more padding and safety straps than an astronaut's rocket seat. It was all more than necessary in Hank's opinion, and Earl's too, by the amused look on his face.

"So, Daddy-Hank, what's with the plane?"

Hank's face nearly went stark white, and he snapped around to see, sure as shit, there she was, sittin' at the dock again.

Earl simply froze, remainin' mute.

Hank flashed a quick glance back to Leanne, tryin' his best not to stutter out a response. "Oh it's— uh— it's a neighbor's plane. His dock is gettin' repairs so he's keepin' it here for now."

She nodded. "Maybe he'll take me for a ride one day." She smiled, threw her arms around him for one last hug, dottin' it off with a kiss, and then dropped into the car.

Earl's arms came around him, huggin' him from behind as they watched Earl's extraordinary daughter pull away, and Hank couldn't be happier. Despite the rough road that brought them here together, he just couldn't be any happier.

Not even the thunder that rumbled over the hills and brought on a light sprinkle, sendin' them inside, could dampen his mood.

6

Earl was in the shower for a quick mornin' wake-me-up. Later, if the storm let up, he planned to go over to meet the new loggin' crew before he started back at work with the new contract next week.

He heard the phone ring and ducked his head out. "Hank! You getting' that?" He stopped to listen, hearin' the phone ring again. "Hank! How 'bout catchin' the phone, will ya?" Again, the phone rang, so he shut the shower off, grabbed a towel on the way out, still leavin' a trail of puddles down the hall as he went after the phone.

"Yeah?" He answered the phone a little louder than he had planned to, but he could hear some strange noise goin' on outside that was draggin' at his attention.

"Hey, Pop, is Leanne up? I was kinda expecting her to be home last night, but I guess you two were just needing some more time."

Earl hardly heard a word, while he scratched at his beard contemplatin' the noise. It sounded like someone was actually tryin' to start that damn plane up. He walked over to the picture window that looked out over the lake, his attention trackin' down the noise. He saw Hank down on the bank, his hands over his head just gawpin' at the banged-up airplane while the prop blades kicked around. The motor sputtered as it seemed to try to start up, then stopped.

"Pop?" David's concerned voice came over the phone again, remindin' Earl he hadn't answered the question.

Earl brought the phone back up to his ear. "Uh, no David. Leanne left last night at about eight thirty, I suppose." He answered, more on autopilot, still watchin' Hank and the plane.

"What? Pop! She didn't come home." David's concern now turned into a loud panic.

Everything inside Earl stopped like a wrench had just been thrown into his chainsaw. He instantly whipped his head turning away from the window scene and zeroed in on the words he heard on the phone. "What'dah ya mean she never made it?"

"Oh Jesus—" David's panic came over the line, *"I— I'm coming up."*

"No wait! Stay there, but start makin' calls. Get Thomas with the sheriffs on the phone. Then call tow trucks and hospitals. Does she got a friend halfway that she might'ah stopped at and forgot to call ya?"

"Uh— n-no, no friends—"

Earl could hear David fumblin' with somethin', most likely pullin' out a second phone. *Phone*—right. *Leanne's cell phone.* "David, have you tried her cell phone yet?"

"Yes, but it goes straight to voice mail." There was a moment's pause and then the question he feared most came to the surface. *"Oh shit, Pop, what if—"*

The plane outside sputtered louder, and finally the engine kicked in, and throttled up to full force. Earl turned back to the window. Five or six times they'd seen that damn thing disappear and come back. Not once had they seen it start its motor. Somethin' was weird, and his baby-girl was now missin'. He couldn't help but think maybe there was a connection. "Start makin' the calls, David. Hank and I will drive Mountain Boulevard and look for her. Keep your phone on you." Earl punched the end button and dropped the phone on the table.

He stared out at the plane— watched as it eased backward in the water, away from the dock, then came back in. Its gear flaps, on its wings, moved up and down, the rudder tail moved side to side. *It was callin' Earl, tryin' to tell him somethin'.* Hank twisted in his spot still down on the bank and looked up toward the house, then back to the plane.

Earl rushed to the door, swingin' it open. "HANK!" He didn't bother with anythin' else, just headed for the bedroom, snatched some overalls and a shirt, grabbed his boots, and headed back out, dressing as he went. Hank was just coming through the door when Earl got his boots on.

"Did you—" Hank stopped in his tracks, his thumb pointed back over his shoulder at the plane and froze in place.

Earl could see that the look he must'ah had on his own face was far more worrisome to Hank.

"What's wrong?"

"Leanne didn't make it home last night."

Hank's face went sheer white, and his knees started to buckle.

"Oh shit!" Earl jumped up, catching him before he actually did go down. "Don't you go south on me now. We're gonna find her. We ain't losin' no more kids, you hear?" Earl tried to sound as firm and certain as he could, but there was no erasin' Hank's past, or the twin boys he lost over the ravine so many years back. They'd just turned nineteen. "Hank." He rattled him up a bit 'til Hank looked at him, *seein' him*. "We're gonna go find her, right now. Get to the garage, grab a couple yarns of rope. Grab a chainsaw too— one of the big ones. And a couple of the big flashlight lanterns. Throw 'em in the truck. I'm gonna grab the radios and a few blankets."

Hank nodded but didn't move.

Earl took Hank's head in his hands and held him tight; forcing him to look at him. "We will find her." They nodded together, and just then— they heard the high-pitched full rev of the plane's engine. They turned both stepping for the door and Earl brushed the creen open wide to look just as she was skiddin' across the water on her pontoons. The plane floated, tapped the surface a few times, like a skipping rock, then lifted off, and suddenly— she vanished.

Earl's heart was doin' double time. His nerves danced over his skin, all coilin' into a central knot in the pit of his stomach. *That fuckin' plane knew where Leanne was, and it was headin' for her now.* "Let's go."

Within fifteen minutes, they had everything they could think of for a rescue operation loaded up in Earl's truck. David had already called back on Earl's cell phone, now under Hank's management, letting them know no one matching Leanne's description or a baby had been brought in to either of the three likely hospitals in the area.

Earl started up the truck, but one look in the rearview mirror had him frozen stiff, all except his hand, slapping at Hank's shoulder.

Hank looked at him, but then his attention snapped to the object behind the truck, making him do a double take— *at the plane that was sitting in the driveway right behind them.*

"What the hell?" Hank muttered, swallowin' hard.

The plane sputtered her engine, the prop blades sped up, and then like a whisp of fog, vanished into thin air once more.

Thunder rolled in the distance, bouncing off the mountains. The lull in the storm was over and the next band had arrived. It was gonna start rainin' again here soon, and the dark, dreary weather was goin' to make it hard to find his daughter if she did in fact go off the road.

Earl threw the truck in gear and stomped the gas. "Keep an eye out for that plane," He growled. Somethin'— he weren't too sure he even wanted to name or say it out loud, but somethin' in his gut— told him to follow that fuckin' plane.

Earl turned southwest down Mountain Boulevard, a long windin' two-lane road that snaked through the highest mountain peaks in the state. There were maybe a dozen spots along Mountain Boulevard where a car could run off and fare little more than a ditch and perhaps a bump on the head. The rest were steep slopes where, if you were lucky, you got snagged in a thick of trees before slidin' down into the lake or droppin' off the side of a cliff.

As the search for Leanne began, they could hear the sputtering engine of the plane overhead. Hank was half-bent-over in his seat, watching out the windshield to keep an eye out for the red stripe along a banged-up body against as an equally grey and unwelcoming sky.

But not two miles down the road, the rain caught up with them.

Earl switched the wipers on high, his eyes scanning the sides of the road for any signs of a runaway. Being summer and having a healthy season of rain, the forests were thick with green leaves and wild shrubs; some spots thick enough to hide a semitruck.

Hank reached over and turned the CB radio on, dialing in on the emergency scanners.

Earl thought he spotted a break in some of the trees, and he quickly pulled over to investigate. "Try her phone again!" He shouted back to Hank as he jumped out and ran to the edge of the trees. Rain came down in pelting heavy drops, beating down on his body, and stinging his eyes as he strained to see past the thick of oaks, pines, hickories, and poplars. Mixed into the dense woods were blossoming mountain laurels that added deceiving color through the breaks of greenery. Looking closer along the side of the road revealed no tire marks or cuts into the ground of any kind to indicate something the size of a car had gone off the road here. The coughing of an engine caught his attention just as Hank was calling out to him from the truck.

"EARL! LOOK!"

Earl already knew, but it still sent his stomach into flips when he looked down the road ahead, and just there, sitting in the middle of it was the plane, facing them. Once more moving its tail flap, revving, and sputtering its motor, telling him enough was enough and stop second-guessin'.

Earl looked up in the dark sky at the low-lying clouds rumblin' with thunderous cracks of rage. Lightning scattered across the sky like shattered glass. His clothes were drenched through and through. Rain like this when the ground was already soft meant mudslides. Just one more thing puttin' his baby-girl at risk. If she was out there alive, time was runnin' out for her.

"Alright, goddammit!" He shouted at the plane. "You take me to her. You find my baby-girl! You hear me!"

In answer, the plane throttled up its engine and vanished.

Earl ran for his truck, jumped in, and took off down the road. He glanced up every so often, lookin' and listenin'. He could see the plane keepin' low, just over the treetops. It pitched and yawed in the storming winds that taxed its single prop motor, but it kept going. Large headwinds threatened to send her up in a climb, tipping her nose over tail, but Earl could hear the engine cut as the plane countered with a nosedive, leveled out, and then throttled back up to keep going.

"Earl Knox, you listenin' in?" Earl's name came over all the standard reports of traffic on the CB radio of downed power lines, and a washout of one of the small back roads near the river. Earl wasn't about to take his hands off the wheel or his second eye off that plane.

Hank scooped up the hand mic to the CB. "Copy that. We're listenin' in."

"Sheriff Kennedy here. David Munro called in said Leanne didn't make it home. We got a search team headin' out your way now, but I can't get a plane or a chopper up in this. I'm sorry, boys. I sure wish I could."

Hank glanced out the windshield, spottin' the ghost plane. It didn't matter; they had their own, flyin' just overhead. Just then, a bolt of lightning split across the sky and struck the right wing of the small plane.

Forgetting the sheriff on the radio, Hank made some fast prayers as he watched the plane drop when its engine cut out, its pontoons crashing through treetops. Hank's heart was thumpin' overtime in his chest, and he couldn't even hear the rest of the details of the Pocono search-and-rescue that was just being launched from the Scranton Sheriff's Station.

The plane coasted overhead, teetering as it struggled to maintain its altitude. The engine coughed and choked, but finally caught, and it popped back up, gaining some safe distance over the treetops.

"Dammit, no!" Earl gunned the truck to keep up as the plane took off ahead of them, disappearing over the next ridge.

Earl careened his neck to look out of the truck, finally rollin' the window down, and stickin' his head out in the spray of needle like raindrops that thrashed his face as he listened for what he could no longer see.

They came around the bend in the road and suddenly the plane was right there in front of them.

"EARL!" Hank shouted.

Earl slammed on the brakes; the truck skidded when the antilocks couldn't catch the soaked wheel drums. Earl jerked the wheel, and the truck drifted sideways as it passed right through the plane. Coming out on the other side of it in a complete 180 turnaround before coming to a complete stop. And as if passing through a ghost plane wasn't shocking enough, when they both looked up, they saw the plane was facing them, just as it had when they came around the bend.

"Hell's fire, what just happened?" Hank whispered.

They both sat motionless in the truck a moment, waitin' for their hearts and stomach parts to catch up with them. Only now the plane was different— as the engine sputtered so did its transparency, fading in and out.

"Earl!" Hank's arm cut across Earl's eyesight, pointing out the driver's side window to a stand of trees that were chewed open, like scars from a fast-moving car.

Earl and Hank both jumped out of the truck and ran to the edge. They couldn't be sure if Leanne's car was down there, but the cut in the trees kept goin'. Someone was down there. "Hank, go ahead and set some road flares. I'm gonna turn the truck so we can—" he stopped, seeing the plane directly right behind them suddenly vanish. Then he heard the sound of a single prop engine sputterin' and cuttin' out. This time comin' from down the mountainside. It was a good hundred yards or so, but they could make out the distinctive sound. "Get the flares, Hank."

They both ran back to the truck. Hank grabbed several road markers from the truck box and ran up toward the bend to set them out, while Earl pulled the truck around, and turned on all the flood lamps that lined the cab. He plugged in the spotlight mounted on the side of his truck and moved it around to shine directly down through the cut of trees. And there it was— the red four-door hatchback Leanne had left in, turned on its side and lodged against a tangle of three or four trees. He only hoped his daughter and granddaughter were still in there alive.

With their location confirmed, Earl picked up the radio and called in. "Thomas, I found her. Just west of the house on Mountain Boulevard, approximately two-and-a-half miles southwest of Timber Trail, in the bend of Two Man's Point Peak."

"Got it. Crews are on the way. Just stay put—"

Earl dropped the radio, not botherin' to argue with the man about not doin' anythin' until they got here first. Leanne was down there, and he was gonna go get her.

"Earl— Earl!" The sheriff's calls over the CB went unanswered.

Earl turned the truck once more, backing the tailgate to the edge of the road. He set the brakes in place and got out.

The rain wasn't lettin' up for anythin', but he knew what to do. Hank was already unwinding the steel cable from the work spool and hooking it into the come-along winch. He dropped the gate and kicked the spool right out of the truck bed, watching as it tumbled down the mountainside. Next, Hank twisted the lamps on the truck cab around to shine down the hill as best as he could, while Earl grabbed up the eighteen-inch circular saw and latched a bit of rope to it so he could tie it to his waist. Both men pulled on their safety harnesses, slung a yarn of rope over their shoulders, and were ready.

"Hang up here for a bit, 'til I get down there. I'll hook the cable to the car and then you can use the winch to pull it up right. Then come down."

Hank nodded to him, tucked a radio in Earl's overalls, and watched from the truck as Earl slowly began to make his way down the slope.

The only good thing with all this was the ground coverage. It was soggy as all get-out, but it had enough runaway tree roots and ground scrub to hold it together. The last thing they needed was a mudslide right now.

"LEANNE!" Earl called out for his daughter, hopin' for a response. Anythin' to tell him there was hope. His only answer so far was the thunder and lightning that continued to roar overhead, and the sputterin' engine of the plane below, callin' him to come quick— *come quick.*

It took Earl about twenty minutes to rappel down the length of rope that ran along with the steel cable, but he finally reached the overturned car.

He made a few side steps, not wantin' to rest on the car just yet. Not until he was sure it wasn't at risk of goin' any further. He grabbed up the cable hook, snapped it in the chassis, and then called Hank up on the radio. "Go ahead and take up the slack, then stop her right there!"

Earl watched carefully as the excess of the steel cable started to move, backwinding its way up the slope until finally it had some tension on it without actually pulling on the car. "Hold it right there!" He called into the radio, and the cable stopped with a slight jerk on the car. And that's when he heard it— a sound that what was meant to be the world's most irritatin' sound, was music to his ears— *his grandbaby's cries*. "I hear you, precious! I hear you!" Tears laughed out as his heart swelled with some relief. "I'm comin'! Grandpop is comin' to get you! You just keep cryin', baby-girl!"

"Can you see them?" Hank's voice came over the radio.

"I hear her!" Earl shouted into the radio. "I hear Crystal cryin'!"

"Oh, thank God. Is Leanne okay, too?"

"Don't know yet. I wanted to make sure we had the car secured in place before I started lookin' around it. Give me two minutes."

"Okay, be careful."

Earl tucked the radio back into his overalls and steadily moved around the car, hopin' to see his baby-girl through the windshield. His chest was ready to explode as he slowly came around the nose of the car. Dirt and broken brambles clogged up the smashed windshield, but the car was lodged against a thick clutch of four trees that had grown into each other and held the car firmly in place. At least it wasn't goin' anywhere, and they would be able to extract his daughter without further risk of slidin'.

Earl braced his back against one of the trees and started pullin' at the branches.

There weren't much left of the roof. What hadn't been crushed on the way down was taken care of by the trees that held it. As he managed to get a thick clump of roots yanked free of the broken glass, he could see Leanne— his baby-girl crumpled over on the bottom of what used to be the passenger side of the car. The cut strap of her seat belt dangled down as if to point the way, which meant she'd a been conscious after the wreck and managed to free herself from her seat belt. He could see rivulets of blood on her forehead, but she wasn't moving. "Leanne!" He shouted.

He punched through the shattered glass, grabbed hold of it, and ripped several sections out until he could finally reach in and touch her. "Leanne! Come on, baby-girl, answer your pop!" Earl could barely reach her, but he managed to brush her cheek with his fingers. Her eyes fluttered open, but only for a moment before closing again. *She was alive. Thank fuckin' God almighty, she was alive. Both his baby-girls were alive.* Now he just needed to get them out and to a hospital.

Earl called up on the radio once more with the order to pull the car over. Earl kept behind it and watched carefully as the cable began to pull on the car. The steel cable creaked and popped while the trees fought to hang on in a tug-of-war, but the come-along won out, and within a few minutes had managed to pull the car back to its wheels.

Crystal's cries came out in frightenin' gulps, demandin' someone answer her.

Earl climbed back around, carefully making his way over mud, rock, and splintered tree trunks, but as he came around, he wasn't seein' the baby seat in the backseat as he expected. Then suddenly there were more lights comin' down from the hilltop. Someone else must'ah seen the truck and stopped.

Earl looked into the backseat, and he couldn't explain for one second the flood of emotions that washed through him, seein' the movement of tiny arms under Leanne's raincoat. Earl reached past the broken glass and lifted the jacket just enough to see his precious grandbaby. And there she was snug as a bug and none too happy, as her little red mouth wailed out, but that damn space-age, overstuffed, baby seat was likely the thing that had kept her safe. That and the swaddlin' of blanket and a raincoat Leanne must have been able to cover her with before passing out herself.

Earl left the blanket and jacket over Crystal until he could get all the glass popped out of the window. He unbuckled her and pulled her from the seat, and then wrapped her inside his bear-hug cocoon. "I gotcha, baby-girl. I gotcha." Crystal just kept on cryin', but he didn't mind a bit. "You just keep on cryin'." He told her, 'cause right now, he loved that sound.

"Earl!"

Earl turned to see Hank comin' down the slope along with two others, Scottie, and his buddy Jacob, who was also part of their loggin' crew.

"We heard the news on the radio, heard your location, so we headed out to see if we could help. Is the baby okay?"

Hank went right past them both and made his way 'round the car, reachin' in to touch Leanne. Earl nodded to Scottie. "Yeah, I think she's goin' to be okay, but we need to get her out of this weather."

"Jacob!" Scottie called to his friend, who came up beside them, and held out one of those baby backpack thingies. *It was perfect.* "Maggie is with us. She can keep the baby while we get Leanne out."

In no time at all, they had the doohickey strapped to Jacob's chest with Crystal loaded up in it. Jacob started the climb back to the top, Earl's grandbaby crying the whole way up.

"What do you need me to do?" Scottie wasted no time gettin' instructions. He knew time was the bearin' element in any rescue, especially when the weather was showin' no signs of lettin' up.

"Let's see if we can get the top of the car off," Earl answered, grabbin' the circular saw he'd brought down with him. "Hank! See if you can get a blanket over her."

Hank nodded, then started pulling more of the windshield out so he could reach Leanne. Once he had all the glass cleared, he unfolded the blanket he'd brought down with him, and covered her up with it.

With a thumbs-up from Hank, Earl started cutting across the crumpled roof of the car along the backseat. Sparks went flying in a rooster tail, both inside and outside the vehicle.

Scottie held the car steady, using the hook of his prosthetic arm to grasp the sharp metal edges. Earl was halfway through the cut when the landscape around them became flooded with flashing colors of red and yellow. *Help had arrived.*

First down was four men from Fire & Rescue. They stepped up right away to assist Earl with the cutting and began to peel the top of the car forward. As soon as there was the smallest amount of space, Scottie crawled his skinny ass into the car, and managed to get over the front seat to where Leanne was. Two arriving paramedics were right behind him, when

Earl finished the first cut, and climbed down off the car.

"She's alive!" Scottie called out. "She's got a strong pulse, too!"

All the adrenalin that was keepin' Earl goin' disappeared with the news, and his knees wobbled under him. Derik, one of the four firefighters, grabbed his shoulder to steady him. "Earl?"

Earl nodded. "I just needed to hear those words." He spoke with a slight warble to them.

Derik nodded his understandin'. "Let us take it from here, and get your daughter out, will ya?"

Again, Earl nodded, and he set the circular saw down just as the rescue team began cuttin' more sections free. Earl could see Hank, his arms still buried to his shoulders inside the car holdin' onto Leanne, while Scottie checked her for further injuries. Earl felt almost numb at the moment. All that fear and rush, and the oddity of the plane— he was grateful, but wasn't goin' to trust it was over, not yet. The plane— he stopped to listen, but it was gone. Nothin'.

The top of the car came free and was lifted away. From there, things happened rather quickly, as paramedics were able to reach Leanne. Sending Scottie out of the way, they began a full examination of her conditions, just as two more rescuers came down with a stretcher.

 Hank was there the whole way. While he was still on the outside of the car, he kept a firm grip on Leanne's hand, talkin' to her, lettin' her know they had Crystal up in the truck where she was safe and dry, and her daddy was just a few feet away.

Paramedics had taken her vitals down, wrapped her head, and splinted both a leg and one arm. In addition, they put a brace around her neck as a precaution, as they prepared to move her from the car to the stretcher. That's when she opened her eyes and looked at him. "Look—" she said feebly.

Hank shook his head. "You're gonna be fine. Don't you worry." He spoke, reassurin' her.

"L-look." She slurred the repeated word. Slowly her splinted arm lifted, and fingers uncurled to point over his shoulder before blackin' out again.

Hank watched as the medics transferred her to the stretcher that would lift her back up the hill where an ambulance waited. He stood wonderin' what she meant and slowly turned, lookin' over his shoulder.

Somethin' a little farther down in the trees captured and reflected back the flashing emergency lights from up top. Hank felt a lump in his throat, which was surely from his heart. *Shit, he already knew he didn't really want to see this.* "Hey, Earl, bring me one of them lanterns."

Earl made his way over, turning the brilliant flashlight on, and aimed it in the direction Hank pointed.

There below was the plane.

Only this time it weren't no apparition. The CF-AYO Norseman was tore up perdy bad and nearly pitched on her nose at an eighty-degree angle. Her wings had been sheared off by the thick of trees, and a broken branch that had smashed through the windshield, protruded out like a foreboding lance. Covered in soot, mud, and vines, it was clear she had been there for some time.

"Derik!" Earl called back over to the rescue crew. "You best come have a look at this!"

Several hours later, Earl and Hank stood back up top on the edge of the road as the crushed section of the plane was finally hauled up the slope, usin' the heavy weight capacity wench from a semi-tow truck, brought in for the job. It was evenin' now, but at least the rain had finally moved on.

Leanne and Crystal had long since been taken to the hospital by ambulance, where David would be waitin' for them, as well as the rest of the family. Earl and Hank knew they couldn't go just yet. Someone had to be here when they pulled the remains of the pilot from the plane. *Their plane.* The plane they had been seein' at their dock and that had led them here. Every detail matched, from the naked sheet-metal body with the red stripe, to the oversized pontoons— right down to the registration number on the tail section, includin' the last four numbers they hadn't been able to make out on it before.

Earl pulled his cap from his head when they opened the hatch door, and he saw the skeletal remains of a man, impaled by the very same branch that'd pierced the windshield. It was at the dark moment, Earl sure wished he had a certain pink baby head to wipe his tears on. This was a tale he wouldn't be able to tell her for some time, but he would. He would make sure she knew about their plane from nowhere— and how it saved their lives.

Epilogue

Earl and Hank weren't expectin' company, so the sound of the car comin' down the driveway had them both stirrin' to their feet and goin' out to see who they owed such honors to. The last person Earl expected to see was his baby-girl, Leanne. Not so soon, at least, after the fright she went through only two weeks ago.

Earl and Hank waited impatiently beside her new SUV for her to unload— *baby-less?*

Earl frowned and peered around his daughter, double checkin" the back seat area for his grandbaby. He gave his baby-girl a disapprovin', pouty scowl. "Where's my grandbaby?"

Leanne just smiled warmly and wrapped her arms, cast and all around him in a smug hug. "I brought someone else this time." She spoke just as warmly as her hug, then leaned back, reached inside the brand spankin' new SUV, and plucked a photograph from the dashboard. She held it up to show Earl.

Earl only looked at it.

"This is René Larouche." She paused, glancin' up at him and then over to Hank. "He's the man you found inside the plane."

Leanne may as well have been hot coals just then, the way Earl dropped his arms, and took a step back. He glanced at the photo she held out to him but waited until Hank was actually at his side before takin' the faded black-and-white photograph.

Some tall, lanky chap stood on the dock— their dock. Earl even looked over Hank's head at the real deal down at the water for comparison to be sure. Sure, as shit, it was theirs. The two slopin' peaks to either side of the horizon matched up perfectly. And there in the water, right behind René Larouche— was their plane. Only in the photo, she was lookin' rather spiffy.

"I asked Sheriff Kennedy to do some snoopin' around. Your plane was registered to one René Larouche from George Rocks, Nova Scotia, Canada."

Leanne went on to tell them the story of her discovery. "He has a logbook of regular flights to, guess where?"

"Here." Hank barely got the word out, soundin' more like the croak of a toad.

Leanne's eyes started to tear up and she nodded. She stepped back and opened the backseat of her new wheels, reached in, and pulled out an ammo box, then handed it over to Hank— and that's when her tears fell. "They found this strapped in the back of the plane's cargo hold. I told Thomas I would bring it up here for you. Turns out your Uncle William had a secret lover. You'll find their love letters and a few photos of them together. René and his plane went missin' around the same time your uncle died."

"Uncle Willie was found floatin' out on the lake. They figured he'd gone out fishin'. Search and rescue first thought maybe he got struck by lightning, but coroners said he'd had a heart attack and died of natural causes."

Leanne nodded again. "I'm thinkin' René went out lookin' for him but got caught in the storm. No one knew he was here or knew where to go lookin' for him."

The lovers' story proved too much, and Earl found his daughter catapulted into his arms again.

Hank clearly wasn't about to be left behind on this one and piled in on the hug as well.

When they had managed to tear themselves apart, they moved to the porch, and took turns readin' some of the letters aloud, laughin' and cryin' 'cause it turned out ol' Willie had his nephew's sense of humor, and René was a bright ol' chap himself.

Before long, Hank abandoned them for his laptop. Earl'd never heard his man's fingers tap away so fast, but he had on account what his Hank was up to. They'd talked about it a few times at night, layin' in each other's arms and tryin' to make sense of it all, when it still didn't.

Now it did. The story was complete. And Earl knew Hank planned on telling it.

Even after Leanne left for home in the security of daylight, Earl stayed out on the porch drinkin' his lemonade and readin' more of the letters. He wondered if there was any ways to claim René Larouche's ashes so they could scatter them here at the lake like Hank had done for his Uncle William's. At least that way, the two would be together again.

Then again, he was sure they already were, with God Almighty.

As the tap-tap-tap sound of keys from his love's first great novel-in-the-makin' continued in the background, Earl kept glancin' down at the dock— hopin' he'd see the plane show up. He smiled 'cause— *she never did.*

THE END

DON'T STOP YET

YOU'RE GONNA LOVE THE BONUS RECIPE
NEXT!!!

Recipe Bonus

CHEESY POPCORN RECIPE

1 Package of black kernel popcorn

{or, for you young folks, one microwave bag of popcorn}

3-4 tablespoons of butter

6-8 tablespoons of Velveeta cheese

(twice as much as butter)

If you're poppin' your corn the good ol' fashion way {like us bears do}, take a large saucepan {or Hank likes to use a deep cast-iron fry pan} and dribble one tablespoon of cooking oil to coat bottom of pan. Then pour kernels in, cover with lid, and raise heat to high.

As soon as kernels start to pop, reduce heat to medium. Shake the pot a few times to let unpopped kernels drop to the bottom.

Listen to the popping (just like that bagged stuff, you young 'n' city folk use), and when the popping starts to slow, remove pan from heat. Go ahead and give it another shake there, for good measure, and pour into a serving bowl.

Hank won't let me melt the cheese in the same skillet, I hate extra dishes, {we're already at two}, so flip a coin on how you want to go about this. But the next step is to melt the butter and cheese together in a saucepan. Stir until it's a soft, gooey consistency, and then pour and mix into the popcorn.

If you're a cheese pig like I am, sprinkle some parmesan for extra cheesy flavor. It doesn't have to be fancy, Kraft will do just fine.

And the last thing— and listen up, 'cause it's really important—

Keep the extra napkins handy or plan for privacy (for finger lickin' exchanges).

Bonus Read

Big Spoon & Teddy Bear

Gay Fiction / Mature-Bear Romance / Sports
Theme / Healing / Adult Content

For years Gage has been turning men into steel, athletes into warriors of strength, competitors into medalists. But Gage isn't looking for any more empty trophies, he's looking for something far more meaningful.

When Gage takes a new job at an old gym, he doesn't expect his entire life to get a workout, just a change of pace. At first it doesn't seem like much and about the only plus is the endless view of rugged and well worked man-candy in the form of weightlifters and Strongman competitors that he'd be training and working with. He figures he has it made the minute he walks in the front door in that sense. But in truth, it isn't enough. He wants a place to set down roots. More importantly, he wants someone to take root with.

Because he's gay, Gage had always been told to just be happy with what he got, but there's something about Boomer. A quiet, towering mountain of a Bear that was the gym's manager who has Gage hoping for more than just daydreaming about the large physique. And that alone promises to put a spark back into the life of a lonely, freckled ginger.

You're never too old for a teddy bear, right?

EXCERPT

Gage held the keys up in his hand, looking them over. Just like that, he was given access to the place. He glanced over at Schiller, unsure how he'd managed to earn the guy's trust so quickly.

"Oh, and one last thing. Stay the hell away from Boomer. Don't get in his way, don't mess with him, and don't go thinking it's your goal to best him at anything. If you do, I ain't gonna bother firing you just to save your ass from getting a beating."

Gage hadn't really meant to ask the blatant question, but once it came out, there was no going back, "Pardon my judgment, boss, but uh, if he's that bad, why have him as manager?"

Schiller pushed back, tipping his desk chair as far as it would go without actually crashing. His arm swung out toward the window behind him and he snatched the cord to the blinds with accuracy and yanked it down. A quick zip exposed the window, putting the gym, on the other side, on display. "See that shit out there? That's every street thug who wants to pack his own guns. Every Latino that thinks he's the next Roberto Duran or Julio Chavez, and every parolee trying to play it straight and they come here to let off steam." Schiller let the cord go and the blinds fell back into place, shutting out the view. The owner glanced at Gage with one of those looks like he had the inside scoop on everything, "Somewhere in all that is a kid trying to make it to the Olympics. *Boomer* keeps the peace."

Gage chuckled, "Maybe he needs a better girlfriend."

Schiller eased back in his chair, rocking, "Wouldn't do him much good. Boomer doesn't fly straight." He smirked, shaking his head mildly.

Gage's gaydar attentiveness immediately perked up, "Boomer is gay and no one harasses him for it?"

It was the owner's turn to laugh now, grabbing his pencil out of habit and scribbled on a pad on his desk, before glancing up at Gage. "Nobody makes fun of Boomer. That is, if the sorry sap wants to keep his car and his body intact."

It seemed like all the bases had been covered in a manner of efficiency and the interview would be drawing to a close here soon and it was just that suddenly Gage wasn't sure he'd landed the right gym for himself. *Street thugs and parolees. Really?*

Gage just kind of slunk down in his seat then, not sure of what he was wanting. He'd left a high paying job working with *Mr. Universe* wannabes and mindless beef-cakes. He came looking for something new— but winding up in some run-down gym for street thug rejects working under a dodgy manager wasn't what he had in mind either. Not even the promising eye candy could make up for this. He wiped across his face just under his nose with the broad web of his thumb and forefinger— thinking it out, but Schiller beat him to the punch.

"Why are you here, son?" He sat back waiting for Gage's answer.

Gage still wasn't entirely sure of his answer. He had grown so numb from all the flash and glam in California. The whole world seemed plastic and generic. Nothing was real or important, nothing fulfilling. Always about more muscle, more glitter, more tanning bronzer, more trophies— but none of them meant *anything*. Having looked out the window while Schiller named off the slummers' flipside version of the same thing, Gage wasn't sure he was going to find whatever the hell it was he *was* looking for here either. About the only good it offered was a job with better Beefy eye-candy.

"Yeah, alright. Why don't you just toss me them keys back?" Schiller sat back up, his chair creaking underneath him as he did, and held his hand out. The disappointment marring the man's aged face.

Gage was reluctant— he still needed a job too.

"This ain't no way station while you look for one of those fancy yogurt gyms. I got boys in here that needs someone to stick it out with them. And I can see right now, you ain't the one."

Gage was certain there might have been more to the lecture, but it was interrupted when someone knocked on the door. The very delivery of *said knock* was like a mayday of urgency from the other side.

"Yeah!? What the hell do ya' want?" Schiller tossed his pencil down and then planted his elbow on his desk, leaning into it, waiting to hear what was on fire.

The door snapped open and a young man's head popped in. "Boomer's in and uhm— well— someone is in his parking space."

Schiller's eyes started to roll across his face like he'd had it with all the nonsense for the day, but then abruptly redirected his focus, leveling it on Gage, "Hope you have good car insurance, son."

That statement was followed by a loud creaking sound of flexing metal coming from outside— then a crash that echoed with breaking glass. The next sound to come from out front was hard to explain, but it sounded like someone was dragging metal across the asphalt.

Gage jumped out of his seat and tore out of the office like his gym-pants were on fire. He crashed into a few bodies along the way until he came stumbling out the front door just as the biggest man he'd ever laid eyes on walked past him with a rather nonchalant gait and went in where Gage had just exited. Gage managed to tear his focus from the towering, pissed-off giant and back to what he feared. But his pride and joy metallic orange Hog was still sitting pretty as could be, right where he left it. The souped-up Honda, he'd parked behind, was another story. No longer where it had been when Gage pulled up. Now it was laying on its side and, if the tell-tale trail of silver paint on the street was any indication, it had been skidded up and out of the marked parking slot. One full car space down.

"Whad'aye tell ya? Fool boy dunne known not to park in the Boomer man's handicap spot."

Gage twisted around seeing the same tall, lean, black guy he'd seen going in when he had arrived. Gage let out another one of those soft huff-like chuckles, so *Fool boy* hadn't been him after all. But rather the unlucky Honda owner.

Like the rest of the sidewalk watchers, Gage herded back in, but he paused just inside letting his eyes readjust and he dialed his attention on the giant now standing behind the counter flipping through the logbook, making a few marks in it, then headed down the hall and disappeared through one of the doors.

Once more, which was like go for three since Gage'd arrived, he was seeing something he couldn't explain, but something about the big silent man had Gage locked solid in a decision to stay. He quickly gathered his thoughts and returned to the boss man's office.

"I'll take it."

Schiller was laid back on his chair, with one of those brand-new tennis shoes propped up on one of the teetering piles of folders, and one solo folder in his hand. "I don't have any positions open for temps. I need someone who can duke it out with these kids. Most of 'em don't have a hope in hell, save for this gym. Don't nobody give a shit about any of these social reject kids. Hell, some of 'em ain't even got caring parents. This gym is their ticket out of here. So I need someone to invest in those tickets." Schiller didn't even bother to look up when he tossed the folder from his hand to his desk and fetched another from a random stack.

"And you'll never find anyone better trained to get them to their goals." Gage sucked in a deep breath with a sound that flared from his nostrils like a bull readying to argue the point.

Schiller twisted around in his chair and dropped the folder from his hand to the desk with a slap. "Give me one good reason why I ought to pick you over all these others?" He waved his hands over the files.

Gage smirked, using the only thing he had. "Because I already have the keys."

IVAN vs. IVAN

Gay Fiction / Mature – Bear Romance / Industrial Blue-collar Theme / Suspense / Adult Content

Out here in the North Sea, love usually passes a man by like a ship in the night. So, it's a nice surprise when the captain of the ship hired to transport Ivan's ocean platform rig into port for the winter might actually offer some unexpected non-business type amenities as well.

Ivan Voloshyn owns and operates the *Marianna Shoal*, a deep-sea oil rig. It's hard work and long days out in harsh weather. And he loves it that way. Because that's what he knows. Seabeds— rigs— oil— and bad weather. He's also about to find out the Norse Gods have a sense of humor. For whom should it be to come riding in on the *Sea Dock* Heavy Lift ship? Another Ivan.

Captain Ivan Blažević knows who he is and what he wants; problem is, he also knows he can't have it. Just because the rest of the world is coming out of the closet doesn't mean every gay man can or should. Out here on the seas, the weather can change in an instant. He needs to trust his crew to do their job, and their hostility towards gays would get in the way of that if he was ever found out.

Ivan-the rig-owner's very presence threatens Blažević's closet doors, nevertheless it's hard to turn that away, because he wants him to keep doing so.

Out here, the North Sea can change a man's life— but hatred can take it away.

THE TEDDY BEAR COLLECTION

Their Plane from Nowhere

Big Spoon & Teddy Bear

Ivan vs. Ivan

TIME: Wounds All Heal

Shaggin' the Dead

COMING SOON TO COMPLETE THE COLLECTION

Life w/ Missing Parts

Chris Kringles' Magic Christmas Socks

About the Twins

We Came— We Saw— and then we took you on an adventure.

Both Proud Indy Authors: Tarian like his twin, Talon, love to torment their editor with a nefarious world of foreign-language, slang, local dialect, stretched/outside-of-the-box definitions, and have even been known to throw in some new word creations of their own at times. This, of course, is all thrown in there with the dyslexia soup stock they both suffer from that makes editing for them a joy {joy: n. see mental illness}.

However, the final product comes out as richly detailed as we believe all stories should be created: holographic worlds of love, pain, frustration, and challenges beyond the every day. We believe a good story should take you on an emotional ride, pluck your heart strings, and zing you about until you're dizzy and screaming at the antagonist, while cheering for the protagonist before returning you to your cozy reading spot. And we've created these adventures within a mix of genres, so you can find the one right for you: Gay & Het Romances,

Suspense, Paranormal and Sci-fi Erotic Romances, War-time Romance Fictions, along with Talon's favorite Space Sci-Fi Frontiers, and Tarian's favorite works of Post-Apocalyptic Dark Fantasies and Historical Fantasies. All for readers to submerse themselves into and escape from their day when they need or desire, and to whet your appetite for more.

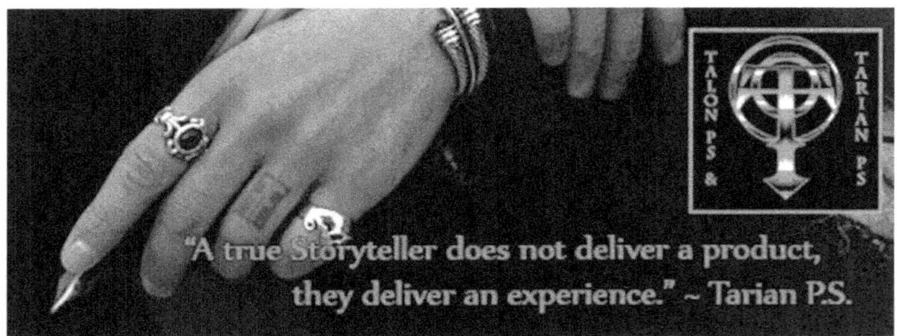

DISCOVER THESE OTHER TITLES BY TALON PS & TARIAN PS

DOMINION OF BROTHERS SERIES
Becoming His Slave
Domming the Heiress
A Place for Cliff
Rough Attraction
Taking Over Trofim
Right One 4 Diesel
Touching Vida~Vince

LA SERIE DES FRERES DU DOMINION – (French Edition)
Devenir Son Esclave - Partie 1 & 2
Dominer l'Heritiere
Un Havre pour Cliff
Attirance Brutale

QUANTUM MATES:
Pt 1~ What Torin Wants

DEAR SOLDIER SERIES:
Dear Soldier, With Love
Dear Soldier, With Love II: A Lost Soldier Named Grey

LYCOTHARIAN COLLECTION:
Bond of the Lycaon Concubine

TALON's KEEP COLLECTION:
Feral Dream by Talon PS
Danny's Dom by Nick Hasse

That's My Ethan

Muse Me Only
Inspire Moi Seulement (French Edition)

THE TEDDY BEAR COLLECTION:
Their Plane from Nowhere
Big Spoon & Teddy Bear
Ivan vs Ivan
TIME: Wounds All Heal
Shaggin' the Dead

THE SADOU ORDER – A Dark Taboo Short
Perfect Boy / Perfect Son

TARIAN ALSO WRITES UNDER THE FOLLOWING PEN
NAMES FOR SEPARATE GENRES:

as STEPHAN KNOX ~ HISTORICAL FANTASY AND
POST APOCALYPTIC SCI FI

Anáil Dhragain (Dragon's Breath)

Keeping With Destiny

as ROCK HARDING ~ ADULT COLORING BOOKS

The Adventures of Hugh Jorgan

CONNECT AND FOLLOW THE TWINS:

www.Talon-ps.com

www.ingramcontent.com/pod-product-compliance
Lightning Source LLC
Chambersburg PA
CBHW061526050726
47593CB00002B/676